UNBROKEN

Book 3 in the FATED Trilogy

Molly Jauregui

Unbroken

Publisher: Absolute Author Publishing House
Publishing Editor: Dr. Melissa Caudle
Associate Editor: Kathy Rabb Kittok
Draft Editor: Natashya Chiles
Junior Editor: Paul S. Dupre
Cover Design: Nick Jauregui

Paperback ISBN: 978-1-64953-328-9
eBook ISBN: 978-1-64953—329-6

Unbroken

"Fated"

Where Destiny is Already Your Past

A Vampire Trilogy

Book III

Dedication

My favorite book of the trilogy, *Unbound*, goes to my littles… who aren't really that little anymore. You fill my days with purpose and keep my heart full. In fact, without my oldest son's love of reading, I wouldn't be on this journey fulfilling my dream. Thank you for picking me to be your mom – Heather, Tristan, Carly, Blake and Wyatt.

My cover artist and younger brother, Nick. You took on a project without hesitation. Your personal dedication and love for your many talents resignates beautiful images on my book covers. Forever grateful for your time and, "NP," replies in getting it done!

A special dedication for the man in my life, Randy McCoy. We have climbed the mountains, and walked the deserts physically and mentally. Some things are just better together and better late than never. Always…

Table of Contents

Prologue

Nonny

The flames of the outer circle of tiki torches grew taller, setting the ambiance, or so it seemed. “No! Absolutely not!” Kirianna, an Elder from the Shadow Night, exploded in anger. As we stood before her, the look on her face reminded me of the old cliché if looks could kill. Tristan stood next to Grant on his right, serving as his best man, both in matching dark suits. Jade stood to my left as my maid of honor, wearing a beautiful, flowing, dark-purple dress. My wedding dress was simple, sleeveless, with an empire waist to hide my ever-growing tummy. Buddy had been sitting behind us, but I wasn’t sure if he was still there. The wind was calm but danced with our dresses ever so slightly. Kiryana had shown up in a long, blazoned, black dress. She scared the crap out of me, for sure. Tearing my eyes away from the angered vampire, I looked over at Grant. I hadn’t known Kiryana had even existed until minutes before. It had been the perfect day concerning all the preparations and excitement for a wedding until about ten seconds ago.

“Binding a nasty human to you, Grant?” Kiryana’s voice was fierce. I hadn’t realized my body was shaking, but now it shook like I was standing in the Arctic, naked. My stomach was churning, and I wanted to throw up. Why wasn’t Grant speaking up in our defense?

“You have to bind them together!” Jade retorted. Finally, someone spoke up!

"Jade, you may be the Queen, but you still have laws to follow, and I'll not break those laws. Especially not for a human!"

Well, that did it! "Quit talking like I'm not even here!" I looked directly at Kiryana, and her gaze met my hostile glare.

"Oh, I know you're here. I smell you like an exquisite port wine newly uncorked, breathing, and waiting to be tasted."

I raised my chin at her, although my shaking continued. Yeah, I was a bit intimidated. Kiryana paused, looking confused. Or, perhaps, she'd just realized the situation. "You're pregnant?"

"Yes," I said sternly.

Her demeanor changed, still cold and scary, but no matter what, I sensed the wheels turning in her beautiful head. The beauty of the vampire race still caught me off-guard, and I couldn't help but stare.

"And Tristan brought me here tonight, full moon and all. He didn't explain why; he just said it was for Jade. Of course, I came for the Queen. Yet here I'm, and now I find out that it is not for Jade, but to bind Grant to a human who is pregnant no less." Kiryana was thinking hard now, and who knew where her thoughts were taking her.

"That is correct, Kiryana." Grant finally spoke up. He squeezed my hand, but it didn't reassure me at all. I continued to shake like a leaf.

"You need to bind them, Kiryana. Nonny and the babies need the protection of the Shadow Night," Tristan explained quietly.

Kiryana's attention focused on Tristan. "Never!" Looking at Grant, she continued, "Ever! Your desperation for a mate is disgusting! To lure a pregnant human into satisfying two needs you desire. A fearless, commanding soldier has gone AWOL?"

"I think that is quite enough, Kiryana! You'll not denigrate my best friend, nor will you denigrate Grant's soulmate and the child she carries!" Jade had stepped forward, demanding the respect of her rank.

Kiryana didn't comply. "I'll not break the law, My Queen."

Again, I had enough. "Actually…" Grant pulled me to his side. Caught off-guard, I didn't finish what I had to say. She had been too stunned to note the plural number of my pregnancy.

"Kiryana, there's a lot you and the rest of the Shadow Night do not know. But, while I'll tell that tale later, I can guarantee you this, not only am I one hundred percent certain I'm standing next to my soulmate, but I'm also sure that the children she carries are mine." Grant finished by placing his hand gently over my stomach.

"Preposterous!" Kiryana exploded, again not noting the fact that there was more than one child.

"It's not! I'm not what you think I'm," Grant challenged.

"That's true," Tristan spoke up. "We were all there when Grant's real ancestry became known."

Kiryana looked between Grant and me and down at the hand still on my stomach.

"What have you done, Grant?" Kiryana sounded like she was in shock.

"Bind us, Kiryana. Please," Grant pleaded.

"This is all wrong! You and you!" she screamed at Grant and me, "are doomed!" Buddy howled behind us.

She looked straight at Jade. "What have you all done?" And with that, she turned and was gone in the blink of an eye.

Chapter One

Mary

Halfway through Nonny's pregnancy, I realized that everything about Nonny's pregnancy hadn't been quite normal for one baby. She was huge early on, and her morning sickness had been worse. I couldn't keep any weight on the poor girl, and all she wanted to do was sleep. When I had told Nonny I thought I had overlooked a second heartbeat, she laughed and threw up on my shoes. "Push, Nonny!" If she would only push through the pain!

"It hurts, Mary!" Nonny cried out. She had been laboring in my bed since early the night before. Nonny hadn't always had a regular menstruation cycle, so the give and take weeks of having twins had to have been calculated correctly. We had figured her due date to be close to March 27th. Twins came early, so we had to take precautions to keep them happy and Nonny's body happy until they would be okay to endure labor and life outside her body. It was now the evening of March 12th. I glanced at the clock on my nightstand. A new day was near, but if Nonny would just push these babies out, they could be born today and not on the unholy date of 'thirteen.'

"Come on, Nonny. You can do it! Let's get these babies out so that we can hold them. I want to see them!" Jade said excitedly. We had gone over delivery procedures a hundred times to prepare for anything that could go wrong. For now, Jade was helping hold one of Nonny's legs and Grant was looking lost and unsure. He stood at Nonny's head quietly. Men! That is why God gave us women all the demanding work. It would be a dead race, or rather races, if it were left up to the men!

Nonny's last contractions had subsided somewhat. "Yeah, Jade. Really? Why don't you crawl on up here and handle this, then? I still have one more, yeow!" Nonny hollered, panting in pain as another contraction started escalating.

"Nonny, calm down and focus. Push with all your might perfect! The baby's head is almost out. Good! Okay, hold on, don't push for a second. I must suction the nose and mouth. A feeling of nostalgia washed over me as I again thought about how I was delivering my grandchildren.

"It's a boy! We have a boy, Nonny! Oh, Grant, come here and cut the cord." I placed the screaming baby on Nonny's still very swollen belly. Jade handed Grant the special scissors to separate the baby from mom. Glancing at the clock, I noted the time, 11:52 p.m. I placed the umbilical cord clamps on and showed Grant where to cut, silently saying a quick prayer that baby "B" was right behind.

"He's perfect, Nonny." I realized Jade was crying in happiness. I looked at her and smiled. Nonny had little time to dote on her little boy as she groaned in pain. Another strong contraction took hold of her body.

"Here, Jade." I scooped my screaming grandson up and handed him to Jade. "Go check him over. Grant, stay here with me just for a minute until Jade is finished. Okay?"

"Yes, okay." Poor Grant was a wreck. His face was stricken with fear. "Is he okay? Is Nonny okay? What am I doing? Is the other baby okay?"

Jade answered over the now-quiet baby. "Grant, good grief, women have babies every day. Everyone is fine, and congrats, Daddy!"

That got Grant to smile for a moment, but then Nonny screamed out in pain. Placing my hand on Grant's hand, I lifted it to Nonny's leg. "Help support her leg the way Jade did." He nodded and did as I asked, but he kept his eyes locked on Nonny's anguished face.

The last baby was almost out. "I can see a golden head of hair, Nonny. Push just like you did before," I encouraged her.

"I'm so tired." Nonny did look exhausted but, at birth, it just didn't matter how you felt until delivery was done

"Your body knows what to do, Nonny. Just help it along." I saw that we only had a couple of minutes left before midnight. If she hurried…

Jade had walked over to Grant to show him his little bundle of joy. "He's perfect, Grant. Take him, and I'll help Mary." She brought her arms forward, encouraging the frightened father to take his son. "You'll be fine. You won't drop him. Show him to Tristan and Mandy. Tristan will be mighty jealous," Jade chuckled.

Grant took the sleeping baby from Jade and carefully walked across my bedroom, exiting just as Nonny grunted and pushed. Jade grabbed her friend's leg.

Time to get this baby out. "Come on, Nonny. Just like last time. You can do this in one push." And with that, a little girl popped out before I even cleared her nose and mouth. She didn't look good. She didn't look good at all. I feared history was repeating itself, as it now stared me in the face, where two are born. It was the curse all over again. I clamped and cut the cord quickly, noted the time, and grimaced. 12:01 a.m. I heard Jade talking but didn't know what she was saying, and Buddy, that dog, was barking like crazy outside the room. Cradling my flaccid, limp baby granddaughter to my chest, I wasn't even sure she was alive. There had been no binding, no Shadow Night wedding. Only one wedding had taken place the weekend after the binding that didn't happen, and that had been a human ritual with Nonny's family. It had gone without a hitch. Her family had been easy to charm and control, and it would continue that way until the day they died.

Kiryana hadn't returned to the Shadow Night either. As requested, Jade and Tristan returned to the palace regularly while Nonny was going through her pregnancy. Kiryana had talked with a few Elders before leaving at Tristan's request. The explanation was that it was time for her to take a sabbatical while things were in order. Several of the others agreed and had planned on leaving for other destinations. It had been a long time since calm had been felt at the Shadow Night. The last time Tristan had gone back, he'd said there was talk about Kiryana and questions about whether anyone had heard from her. With Jade away most of the time, the training had stopped, and the palace just sat in a state of limbo. Grant had refused to leave Nonny's side, even though they lived with me, so he rarely left for his palace duties.

Other than the usual twin pregnancy issues, the last eight months had been too easy. It took holding this precious baby in my arms to realize all wasn't right. Closing my eyes, I said a prayer.

Everything around me went quiet. I opened my eyes and found myself in a place that I recognized. The fire before me was only embers, but the area seemed quite bright, and the smoke people sat on logs behind it, and behind them even more, stood. The entire tribe must have been there.

The Chief spoke. "The boy. He okay?"

"Yes," I answered quickly. "But she is not."

"She? Hmm." There were many sidelong looks amongst the tribe. They had not known the sex of the second baby. They probably had presumed it to be a boy as well. But, of course, the twins in the past had always been male.

"Can you help her? I mean, two have always survived, right?" I questioned.

He was shaking his head. "No. Baby die. Baby born dead. But always, boys. This I do not know." He pondered before speaking. "I feel her now. She lives. I see her now. The gods have spoken. Bring her to me. Her day of birth is not a bad one. It's a separation to survive." I walked carefully around the embers, not feeling any signs of life as I held the baby close to me still. I think he was referring to that she had been born on a different day from her brother. But, with thirteen always being the cursed number. It was all so confusing. And I knew asking for any answers from the smoke people was useless. I would've to figure it out in my own time.

The Chief held his arms out for me to give my granddaughter to him, and I complied. "Boy, steal her life. Universe is unsettled. She is a gift, yes, universe unsettled," he said sadly.

He looked at the highly decorated tribe member beside him. "Cheenahwa… ooph." He nodded his head upward, and the man walked away. The Chief stared at my granddaughter. "Yes, no breath she has. Is near." He reassuringly looked at me. Was he saying she was dead? How was that okay, and what was nearby? All I saw was my granddaughter, and she didn't look alive. But she didn't look completely dead either. I had to be in some state of shock, not to be reacting. This wasn't real. The tribe member who had left reappeared with a brilliantly colored pipe, which he held toward the Chief.

"Ooph, la nay-hawa," The Chief said to him. The other man nodded, and another member came to his side. She carried what appeared to be a palette of colored paint.

It was all tranquil as the Chief put his lips over the pipe. Closing his eyes, he inhaled deeply. Holding it in for a moment, he then blew the smoke up and down the body of my granddaughter. Reaching out, he took two fingers and dipped them in paint. I couldn't hear him very well, but he was talking in his dialect quietly. Across the baby's forehead, down her cheek, neck, and body to the very tips of her toes, he painted the colors of purple and black on her.

I stared at her toes where he'd ended, not realizing that my granddaughter's eyes had opened. The Chief raised her head to his lips and, surprising me, kissed her gently before handing her to me. Once back in my arms, she wailed as no baby had ever wailed before.

I lost it and started crying, cradling my sweet granddaughter to me. None of this made sense, but this precious baby was very much alive.

"Thank you! Oh, thank you so much." I cried to the Chief.

"It not my will. Universe unsettled. You see. Things not right. It done before. You see. No protection. You do what you have to do." He spoke to me seriously.

"You understand? You protect?" he asked.

"Yes, I understand." Unfortunately, yes. I understood somewhat. It was done before. I wasn't sure what he meant about that part, though. It was all about protection, and I guess I would "see" when I was supposed to "see." I was the Oracle in some form. The more time I spent with the vampires of the Shadow Night, the more I just knew where things were and how things should be. I had a direction now, where I needed to go, and what I needed to do. Closing my eyes, I feared that history would keep repeating itself. But I still didn't understand why.

I heard Jade now, so I knew I was back in the room with her and Nonny.

"Let me take her from you, Mary, so that I can check her out, too. Nonny still needs you. Goodness, little girl, you have a set of pipes on you." Jade lifted the baby from my arms, and I saw the colors painted on her from head-to-toe moments ago were gone.

I finished helping Nonny with the rest of what needed to be done. The poor girl was exhausted. I hadn't even heard Grant, Tristan, and Mandy return to the room with my grandson. Instead, they stood by Jade, looking at the little girl. Buddy hung in the doorway, still not sure if he should come in or not. Mandy hadn't wanted to be in the way, and Jade hadn't wanted Tristan to be by himself, so Mandy had hung back with him.

"Bring them both to me," Nonny croaked out. "I haven't even gotten to see my baby girl." Jade wrapped her charge and brought her to Nonny with Grant on her heels, carrying their son. The babies were placed in the crook of each of Nonny's arms.

"They are perfect," she whispered and gently kissed each of them on the forehead.

"Looks like little man got a few more meal servings in there," Tristan joked. But he was right. The boy appeared twice the size of the girl.

"What are you going to name them?" Jade asked.

Nonny looked at Grant for him to answer. "Well, if they had both been boys or girls, that would've been easy. So, I guess we need to pull a name from each side." He looked at Nonny. "What do you think, Mama?" Nonny beamed.

"If I could just cut in here and rain on your parade a moment." Now there were several sets of eyes directed at me. This might be difficult to divert them from the names they wanted, but I needed them to choose the names I had for them for reasons they didn't need to know right now.

"Well, I just thought that with the way things are, it might be a good idea to give them names with the power to do good."

"I don't mean to sound unappreciative of what you just did, Mother; however, I think we, as the parents, should be able to name our children." Grant sounded quite cross. Nonny agreed with him, nodding.

I clasped my hands together at my chest in silent prayer and continued, "If I may just strongly request, on behalf of some wiser and higher people here in the room, to help name these unprotected, and may I add, precious, grandbabies of mine?" I wanted at least some part of what I'd said to stick in a vampire's mind who would understand.

"No," Nonny insisted. "I want to name him," nodding to the little boy. "Christian, and her," she nodded to the other. "Hope. I think those are great names and mean enough." She looked at Grant, who was now scratching his head and looking between the two of us. "Right, Grant?"

"Well..." He was stuck, and he knew it.

"Well, what? And again, Mary, I mean you no disrespect because of your loyalty as the Oracle to the Shadow Night, but they are our children." Nonny was trying to keep the moment light.

"Nonny, if the woman who was once over the Shadow Night, saving us all, is strongly requesting a name for the children, I think you should listen." Tristan threw in his two cents.

Nonny looked at Mandy and Jade for help. They both shrugged. "I don't want to get involved. You both have valid cases," Jade answered.

"So you all are saying I don't have a choice?" Nonny pouted.

Grant sat down on the bed with Nonny. "While I would love to stand up and defend the names we chose for them, I'm hearing the reasoning behind what Mom is saying. We don't have protection. We don't know what is out there. We don't know what will become of our precious little ones. So if there's a calling for chosen names, well, let's hear her out."

Nonny peered past Grant. I guess that was my cue. "Well, first, I would like to tell you the meaning of the little guy's name. The energies this gemstone gives are vital, Nonny. Protection, purification, power, healing. He should be named Jet." Nonny didn't budge. It didn't even look like she was digesting it, so I continued to my granddaughter. "The gemstone chosen for our sweet girl is Amethyst because the stone has been valued for centuries because of its mystical healing properties, stimulating and purifying all the energy in the mind, body, and soul. And so, she will be," I finished, sitting at the foot of the bed as I had just given the speech of my life. It very well could've been.

The room was noticeably quiet, with a tiny grunt here and there from one of the babies. All gazes remained on Nonny, and Nonny's gaze remained on me for what seemed an eternity. Eventually, her eyes needed to adjust and blink, and she did so, looking from one baby to the other. We all waited on pins and needles.

"Okay," she whispered, and looked up with a smile. The room erupted in cheers, evidently much to the babies' dislike, as they both cried. She gave Amethyst to Grant for comfort so she could quiet Jet down.

"Okay then. I'm going to let you guys have some alone time. Nonny, you need to feed those babies. Let me know if you need anything." I had to get out and do some thinking. "I'm going to go write all this down, including the fact that Mr. Jet was born at eleven-fifty-two p.m. and Miss Amethyst came into the world at a minute past midnight."

"Separate days?" They all asked me in unison.

"Yes. Separate days."

"That's interesting." Tristan was thinking about that. Was he questioning the significance? Did he know something, too? His look changed to acceptance.

"I think it's cool," Jade said as she wrapped her hand around Amethyst's tiny hand.

I watched Jade's face change from joy to confusion. "Too cute." Her tone was monotone.

"Okay, well, I guess we're out of here, too. I'll leave the door open a bit if you need something." Jade withdrew her hand, still looking a bit confused but trying to hide it. She took Tristan's hand and tried to pull him toward the door.

"I don't want to go, yet," Tristan pouted.

Buddy whined at the door. "Yes, you do, and yes, you are. Let's go take Buddy outside for a bit," Jade directed Tristan.

Tristan finally turned in response to Jade's tug. And I heard him whining about when it would be their turn to hold the babies. "Come on, Buddy." Tristan patted his leg, and the dog followed them out.

"Well, I'm off to bed myself. I'll catch you all in the morning. If you need me to run to the store before I come back to Mom's house, just let me know." Mandy yawned and gave the babies each a kiss goodbye and was gone.

Clasping my hands together, I checked on the babies one more time. "I won't be far should you need anything or if anything...." I wanted to say "Happens" but thought a better choice of words might be less problematic for the new parents, "comes up."

"We'll be fine?" Grant's question was aimed at Nonny.

She replied, looking sleepily at me, "We'll be fine. I'll attempt to nurse them both."

"Okay then." I left the room, feeling quite unsettled. First the babies, and now something with Jade.

They didn't know, but that was probably a good thing! I needed time!

* * *

The house was finally settled. Of course, it wasn't like everyone was down for the night, as Mandy, Nonny, and I were, of course, the only ones that could sleep. Nonny hadn't become half-vampire through the pregnancy, so she was truly exhausted after the birth of the twins. The babies seemed to be calm and slept for brief spurts. Nonny nursed them, and they appeared to be satisfied with that, for now. A heavy sigh escaped me. True, Grant was my son, and he had behaved the same way. But I hadn't been a part of his life for very long when he had been taken from me. Unfortunately, not all my memories were in my mind to retrieve and understand.

I sat rocking in my chair in the study for what seemed like a very long time. I had to figure out the master plan for my grandbabies, and it seemed my mind always went back to binding whatever grew within them, good or bad. It wouldn't be fair, but I just didn't see any other option. It would be a protection for them as well. They would appear as normal babies to anyone around them if all went well with the spell. Whatever the smoke people meant about Amethyst would be hidden as well. Would this be the best way?? Another sigh escaped, and I stood and began pacing the room. Things were getting so complicated again. I thought about my past as the Oracle and the children. How had God chosen me? Why did I have to make these tough decisions? What if I chose incorrectly? Jade had been returned to the Shadow Night. I had been returned as myself, Mary. Right? Or was it all backward? What if...

There was a soft knock on the door. "Mary? Mom?" It was Grant.

"Come in, Grant." I welcomed the interruption because my mind was so unclear!

"Hey, I just wanted to tell you thanks for everything. Nonny and the babies are doing great." He beamed with pride.

"Of course! It was easy. As Jade stated before, women have babies every day." I wanted to sound upbeat and happy, and I walked over and gave Grant a big hug.

"You look tired. Not Nonny tired, but I'm sure you're due for some rest." He rubbed my sore back as we stood near each other.

"I will get some rest, soon. I'm just reflecting on the birth of my grandbabies and you becoming a daddy yourself." I lied, showing a tired smile and yawning. "Go back to your family. I'm fine, the delivery was a breeze, and all is well." I lied, again.

"Okay. I think Jade and Tristan have gone out for a bit, so they aren't tempted to bug Nonny and the babies too much. Can Buddy hang out with you tonight? He doesn't seem to want to be around the babies yet. I think he's jealous."

"Of course, he can. Where is he?" Just like the dog knew we had been discussing him, he entered the room and jumped up on the sleeper sofa I had pulled out the night before.

"Guess he knew," Grant said, scratching his head. We both laughed. Buddy's head was lying on his front paws, and his eyes were arched up, looking at us.

"Smartass," Grant told Buddy. The dog closed his eyes in response.

"Let me know if any of you need anything, then. Anything at all." I wanted to make sure that they would come to get me raising no questions if anything out of line happened.

"Got it. Of course. We are both new to this whole thing, so don't worry, you'll be the first one I come to." Grant reassured me.

"Okay." I faked a yawn.

"Night, Mom."

Grant gave me another quick hug before he left the room, closing the door behind him. I looked over, expecting Buddy to be fast asleep, but he had one eye open, watching me. I walked over and sat on the bed next to him. His ears went up like he was listening, but he still only kept one eye open.

"Well, you're going to make it a little more difficult for me to perform a miracle tonight. You'd better keep quiet and just go to sleep, Buddy boy," I told him, stroking his head and back. Like I wasn't stressed out enough, having to come up with the perfect binding ceremony. Now, I had to keep a dog quiet if things got a little out of hand.

I headed to the library wall, where I had hundreds of books shelved. I pulled out several on a lower shelf, exposing a hole in the wall where an ancient bound book hid. A safe might have been a better place for the book, for sure, but if anyone were looking for it, I felt they would look for a safe as well, not a hole behind some books. I took the large leather-bound book over to the desk and sat on my chair in front of it.

There was enough dust on the book that I took a hanky from the top drawer and wiped the front of the cover off just so I could read the engraved words on it, *Shadow Bound.* As far as I knew, I was the only holder of such a book anymore. The others must have been destroyed or taken by Keegan the night of the brutal attack. Otherwise, the Elders would've known a lot more about what was going on and about Grant. My book was most likely the smallest of them all. I didn't write what spell, or magic, was used for what. My book was a book of the Oracle. But I knew there was a binding spell of sorts in there. It would just have to be tweaked a bit for its purpose here.

I traced each letter with my finger, slowly, mythodically on the book cover. I always did. It wasn't like it had anything to do with anything within the tome. Perhaps it just made it feel real to me, I guess. I could feel Buddy's eyes on me.

"Go to sleep, Buddy," I whispered, not taking my eyes off the book and getting a soft woof in response. It was great that animals were highly intuitive. I just didn't want him to be that way right now!

"Okay, Mary, let's see what we have to do," I murmured to myself. Buddy softly woofed again.

Chapter Two

Mary

This would not be easy; that was certain. The spell I located in the book for binding wasn't precisely as I'd hoped. As far as what was needed even to perform the complicated thing, I lacked one essential part. It was a part of the Shadow Night, and I wasn't there. I also had to mark the babies before performing the spell, which I'd already planned on while kissing them goodnight. Telling each of them that I chose them might seem awkward to hear, as far as Grant and Nonny were concerned, but I would fumble through that part as well. I could get the Shadow Night here with the essence crystal. I had to hope none of the Elders would be in the ritual room when I conjured the binding of the Shadow Night to hold fast the babies and whatever was within. It was a potent spell. Even without the written word, I would have to add. I would also have to allocate a protector who could not be a relative.

He slept on my makeshift bed. Buddy would be perfect; I looked at him in deep thought. He was intuitive, and even though he seemed to have a problem right now with the babies, he would get over it. Clapping my hands softly together in a bit of excitement, I accidentally woke the poor boy up. Buddy looked at me sleepily for a moment, perhaps making sure I hadn't set the house on fire or put a hex on him. Then, satisfied, he put his head back down and went back to sleep.

I would worry about the writing I had to do shortly. First, I needed to mark the babies and get the small essence crystal from my jewelry box in the bathroom attached to my bedroom.

Quietly, I rose from the chair and walked past Buddy. He raised an ear at me. “I’ll be right back,” I whispered as I left the study and began to closed the door behind me. Buddy opened one eye before I got the door fully closed. I swear the look of knowing what I was up to was there.

As I walked down the hall to my bedroom, I heard a quiet conversation between Nonny and Grant, but the babies were both silent. They had cried little at all since their birth content in the arms of their parents, I presumed. Smiling to myself, I knocked softly.

I heard Grant’s footsteps cross the room before he opened the door. “Hey, Mom, what’s wrong?”

“Nothing. I wanted to give my new grandbabies a kiss goodnight before I hit the hay for a while. Unless, of course, you needed me?” I hoped they were still okay on their own, for now.

“We’re good, Mom. Come on in. The babies are so good. Eating and sleeping a little here and there. Amethyst seems to sleep better...” He let the last of that comment trail off, probably wondering if she was more human, perhaps, than her brother.

“That’s good. I’m sure it will take time for their little bodies to adjust to being outside of their mama.”

And after I get them bound, they will be safe, I told myself. *All will be well then.*

While I walked over to the babies, my stomach flip-flopped a few times. *Please let this go all right*, I prayed. Nonny was asleep holding a sleeping Amethyst. Jet was lying next to her, wrapped in a blue blanket but looking around.

“I was holding him, but when you knocked, I sat him down for a minute,” Grant explained.

“It’s okay,” I chuckled. First, Grant was scared to hold the babies, and now he was making excuses to hold them. Men were so complicated! “You’re a daddy. You can hold your babies, son.”

Grant reached down and picked Jet up and placed him in my arms. "Thanks."

Jet was a handsome little boy. He had a lot of long black hair for a baby. It made him look older than he was already. I walked with Jet to the window and whispered in his ear, "I'll mark you," and placed a gentle kiss on his forehead. His face scrunched up, and I could tell he was going to exercise his vocal cords. Quickly, I walked back to Grant as Jet cried. "I guess he doesn't want to be away from his daddy, yet." I felt my face getting hot and embarrassed that Jet had cried when I held him.

Grant took the baby. "He's probably hungry. These guys seem to like to eat more than anything. I hope Nonny can keep up with the demand."

"What's wrong?" Nonny was groggy, still but awake. She kissed Amethyst and handed her to me. "Let me see the little man. He doesn't give me much rest, I swear. Grant's right, though. I don't know how I'm supposed to keep up with these feeding demands. I thought newborns slept a lot."

Nonny yawned and brought the crying baby to her breast. Jet latched on immediately and was quiet. "He's going to suck me dry and leave nothing for his sister."

That struck a chord with me, as it was probably an accurate statement. The smoke people would not be wrong about anything, unfortunately. I looked down at my sleeping granddaughter. She was so sweet and beautiful as well. How could anything terrible have anything to do with these innocent babies? Maybe, just this once, the things that the smoke people knew were incomplete.

Carrying Amethyst to the window, as I had Jet, I whispered near her ear, "You're marked." I placed a firm kiss on her forehead to ensure she was covered and make myself feel better. She didn't awaken or cry, and I was thankful for that!

"Here, Grant." I placed Amethyst in his arms. "I need to get something from my bathroom, and then I'll leave you all in peace. Remember, there's formula for the babies if you need it," I reminded both of them.

"I know. I don't want to use it, but I won't starve them either," Nonny stated as she stroked her son's hair while he nursed.

Disappearing into the bathroom, I opened my large jewelry box next to my vanity. Then, opening a small drawer, I found the essence crystal. "I hope you're ready for this," I told the object; tucking it into the light jacket I had put on in the office earlier, I headed out of the bathroom and made a beeline for the door.

Grant and Nonny sat next to each other. One baby sneezed as I opened the door, and I heard Nonny ask Grant to get a wet wipe so she could wipe Jet's face because he had sneezed out a mouthful of milk.

Closing the bedroom door behind me, I leaned against it. One task was done, now on to the rest. I quietly walked back to the office and let myself in. Buddy sat on the bed, very much awake now.

"What?" I asked him as I made sure the door closed and clicked behind me. A locked door would be better for the rest of the ritual.

I still had to do a little writing, but I now had everything in this room that I needed. "Including you," I told Buddy. He jerked his head around and let more air out than any kind of bark. "Well, glad you agree." Striding back to my office chair and sitting down with the book still open to the binding spell, I found some paper and a pencil and began writing. Fortunately, the words spilled out quickly, and I silently prayed I had covered my bases with everything that needed to be said and in the correct order. Of course, I had no one to double-check anything, so the pressure was all on me.

Buddy came over to my chair as I was writing. "You ready, Buddy?" I gave his neck a good rub. He continued to lean in, wanting more, and seemed to be sorely disappointed when I stood up and left him for the locked cabinets under my display case of mystical figurines, gemstone rocks, and such. The key was inside a hidden compartment attached to the display case. Pushing on the right area of the cabinet caused a small drawer to pop out with a key hidden inside.

Unlocking all the lower cabinets in front of me, I pulled out three large clear crystals. I had many, but three were all I needed tonight. I had many odds and ends of items I might need to complete a spell or ritual one day. Grabbing a roll of pink and blue ribbon, I still had to decide what to use for the Shadow Night Crystal. I needed a piece of black fabric big enough for all the crystals to sit on. I found some folded up behind a few wands, one of which I would also need. Wands were used merely as pointers. They held no power but were still a necessity. I still lacked something to represent the Shadow Night Crystal. While looking up pensively, my gaze went to the figurines in the case. Buddy was at my side, panting and leaning against me again. "Perfect." And it was. Unlocking the windowed case, I pulled out two mystical figurines. One resembled a dog, and the other was a likeness of the main Palace of the Shadow Night.

I carried my supplies over to my desk in a couple of trips, with Buddy following me both ways. The office room was not spacious, given its furniture, and his anxious pacing with me was more of an obstruction than anything.

"Oh! I almost forgot to mark you. I guess you being in my way was on purpose, huh?" Kneeling, I took Buddy's face in both my hands and told him, "I choose you, Buddy, as protector." Then, as I did to the babies, I kissed his head and got a big, wet tongue on my face in return.

"Ew, Buddy. Your kisses are a sweet gesture, but so gross!" Whispering to him loudly. Then, standing up, I wiped my face with my shirtsleeve.

The desk was in disarray, with items that needed positioning. I scooted everything from the middle off to the side, and placed the black fabric down first. Next, I took each ribbon and put them on top of the fabric, with enough room for the crystal representing the Shadow Night to fit between the two crystals representing the babies. Then, I placed a crystal on each ribbon and one in between. Finally, I set the figurine representing the protector behind the Shadow Night Crystal and the figurine representing the Shadow Night itself behind him.

"Looking good so far, Buddy?" I asked the dog, who had gone back to sitting on my bed and watching me intently.

I pulled the small essence crystal from my pocket and touched each object with it, saying each time, "I choose you," before setting it down in front of the Shadow Night Crystal.

Pulling the book and the paper with my writing toward me, I was finally ready. Picking up the wand, I said a personal prayer to the Higher Powers for their protection and strength.

"Let's begin...."

* * *

I heard Tristan calling down the hallway. "Hello? Where is everyone?" The lights had all gone out, and we were all in various rooms of the house, in the dark. I had forgotten about Tristan and Jade! I heard Grant speaking with them somewhere in the front of the house. Both of the babies were crying as well. I hoped it hadn't been a painful experience. I couldn't imagine…

Buddy whined as well. "Buddy," I whispered.

Fumbling in my top desk drawer, I found a flashlight. Switching it on, I found Buddy crouched next to the door, wanting out.

"Come over here. It's okay," I coaxed him. His tail wagged once, unsure, but he complied.

With him at my side, I listened to the commotion still going on in the house. "I have to hurry and get this stuff put away." Opening a large bottom drawer, I quickly placed everything inside and shut it.

A knock on the door made me jump.

"Mom?" It was Grant, and he was trying to open the door. "Mom, I can't get in. Are you okay?"

"Of course, darling! I grabbed my emergency flashlight. The breaker must have flipped. Is there a storm outside?" Hurrying along, I made it to the door and opened it. "I'll go flip the breaker back. It sounds like the babies need you. Why don't you go back and help Nonny with them?" I knew exactly how I sounded -- guilty!

"Wait, a minute. What's wrong with you? You're shaking like a leaf and jerking around like a crazy person." Grant held me back, using my arm. "The babies and Nonny are fine. Tristan and Jade are in there with her."

"With the births and being stirred out of deep sleep, I'm jittery, that's all. You know how you wake up and don't know where you are?" Yep. I said that to a vampire. Grant was utterly silent for a moment and then burst out laughing. That was a close call.

"I cannot believe you said that. I don't remember what it was like to sleep when I was younger, to be honest." Grant was still laughing.

"See! I'm delirious. Now, let me flip the breaker. Buddy can come with me. Buddy?" I called out. He was already at the front door. "See, my knight in shining armor is already waiting for me." Grant let go of my arm.

"Okay, then. Perhaps when the lights come back on, your mind will be with it." He laughed.

"Probably wishful thinking," I commented.

"Grant?" Nonny called for him.

"Your wife wants you. I'll be right back." Reassuring him once more, I turned and walked toward the front door toward Buddy.

His leash hung next to the door, and although we only used it when taking him into town or somewhere, I attached it to him under the circumstances.

"Don't be dragging me along anywhere, Buddy. You behave and stay with me." He whined in response, wanting the door to open immediately.

With a bit of tugging and sweet-talking, Buddy quit trying to make a run for it and walked next to me to the breaker box. I opened it, stood to the side, and flipped the breaker back on. The house and porch were illuminated once more.

I let Buddy do his business, and then we headed back inside. Buddy stayed behind me in the house, but he followed me into my bedroom, where everyone still was.

"It looks like lips." Jade said before laughter sounded from them all. The babies had finally calmed down. Jet, as usual, was being nursed by his mom, and Jade had Amethyst lying in her lap.

"Hey, Buddy," Grant acknowledged the dog. "Are you finally coming in to take a peek?" Buddy, with a wagging tail, went to him for attention.

"Look, Mary," Jade said, motioning me over. "It looks like Amethyst has a tiny birthmark. You see it? It's light, but it looks like a set of lips. That's what we're all laughing about."

Nodding, I agreed that yes, I could make it out. But, of course, I knew whose lips they were! "Yes. Kind of, I guess." I wanted to play it off. "Babies get many birthmarks in various places. Eventually, they fade out, though." I hoped!

"Does Jet have one?" Jade asked Nonny.

"Uh-uh. I already checked. Maybe just a speckle here or there, but nothing with any shape," Nonny replied.

Uh-oh. What did I do wrong? If Amethyst had one, then Jet should've one. Feeling a bit panicked, I looked at Buddy. He was next to Jade, smelling Amethyst. That was an excellent sign. But we had to be two for two. Like he knew I was watching him, Buddy looked over at me, and I swear on the top of his head, I could see a few changed colors of the fur on his head in a very recognizable shape (if you knew what you were looking for), lips, he had them, too. But not Jet.

"Can I burp Jet for you, Nonny?" I needed to look for myself.

"Sure, here." Nonny handed Jet to me. He seemed sleepier than he had several hours ago. That was a good sign. I put him up to my shoulder without trying to make what I was doing too conspicuous. I hadn't been able to get a good look. The more human, the less concerned I would be. I took him over to the window, trying to get him to burp. Come on, little guy, burp so I can look at you. And he finally did.

"That was a good one," Tristan exclaimed.

"Takes after his dad," Grant said proudly, setting off another chuckle through the room.

"I think he needs a diaper change, Nonny," I told her as I walked back past them and over to the changing table we had set in the room last week so the babies could be checked over after birth.

Jet slept, even after I laid him down on the diaper-changing mat. I looked his forehead over, and as Nonny said, there wasn't much. As I changed his diaper, I concentrated on remembering the sequence of events from when I was in the room earlier to mark them. I did the same to each, and Jet had sneezed milk all over himself, and the mark was washed off. I stood with his new diaper half-on and half-off, unable to move. I had been so careful! I'd done everything in order and had said the right things!

"He's going to pee on you if you don't finish the job, Mom," Grant said as he stood next to me, watching.

"You're not telling me something?" It was a question more than a statement.

Should I tell him? Should I say something? "Just caught off-guard again. I can't believe that after so many, many years, I have had no one except

Mandy, and now I have you all." Finishing with the diaper, I wrapped Jet back up and held him in my arms.

"He is something, isn't he?" Grant was a proud daddy. He stroked his son's cheek.

"He sure is. You have two healthy children and a soulmate. That's what life is about." Nodding my head, a tear escaped my eye.

"You're crying?" Grant asked quietly.

"Well, it's about time some emotions got a chance to run, don't you think?" I smiled through a few more tears.

"Absolutely." He hugged us both. Jet opened his eyes. Again, he looked older than he was.

"Here. I need to get some sleep. The sun is going to rise soon, and I want to get some rest." I did. I hoped that sleep would bring answers.

"Okay. You sleep as long as you need to. Mandy will be here, I'm sure, at the break of dawn. Tristan and Jade are here. We've got this covered." Grant reassured me this time.

"Okay. Night all." Waving, I left the room. This time, Buddy stayed with the group. I went back to my office and climbed onto the sleeper sofa bed, hoping sleep would overtake me. I lay there, saying many prayers that Jet was protected and that the binding on him was complete. With no way of finding out. All I could do was wait and hope my dreams would bring me the answers.

When sleep came, it wasn't filled with answers. It was like I was watching a movie about the day's happenings. First, the births of the babies, and the glitch of being with the smoke people. Then, I saw myself kissing each baby, Buddy, and then retrieving all the needed elements for the spell. My life's events played in a fast-forward movement. Lips moved, but there were no voices, right up to where the three crystals were lit up while I was saying my written words with my gaze on my paper and not on the crystals--the moment right before the lights had gone out. Then it felt like a pause button had been pushed. In the crystal marked for Amethyst, her sleeping face was there. The crystal marked for Jet was a silhouette, I hoped, of him. The middle one representing the Shadow Night; that one was full of angry Elders looking straight at me.

I woke up in a cold sweat, panting and looking around.

"Oh, Mary. What have you done?"

* * *

The babies were growing every day. Nearly a month old, and I still was no closer to having an answer about what had happened that night. They slept a lot, just like human babies did, and because of that, I was hopeful. Buddy was always near Amethyst, and his barking at Jet had stopped. I felt like he was watching over them both. I could be wrong. I had been wrong before.

No one had gone back to the palace since the births, but it was certainly on everyone's minds. My nerves were about shot to pieces, expecting the Elders, soldiers, anyone, to show up from the Shadow Night. They had to be close. I could feel it in my bones. Tristan and Jade stayed here with Mandy, so we weren't all feeling on top of each other.

I watched Jade prepare dinner in my kitchen. It was something she had gotten into the habit of doing over the last month. Of course, she didn't eat it, but she certainly enjoyed making things up for those of us that could.

There was still a chill in the mid-April evening air, but spring was near. I couldn't wait! Bringing the yard out of hibernation would be a lot of work, and I welcomed it with open arms.

Mandy was in my bathroom with Nonny, helping her bathe the little ones. Grant and Tristan had gone out for the night hunting and whatever else they did when they went out all night.

A crash pulled me from my thoughts. I had been watching Jade, but I was lost in a daydream. She was sprawled on the floor, looking at the ceiling.

"Jade?" Jumping from my seat at the table, I ran over and kneeled next to her. "What happened? Are you okay?"

"Where am I?" she said, trying to sit up.

"In my kitchen making dinner, as you do every night." I was concerned about her confusion.

Mandy came quickly around a corner with Amethyst wrapped in a towel, and Nonny was close on her heels with Jet also wrapped in a towel. "What happened? Jade? Why are you on the floor?"

"I… I do not know." Jade sounded very confused. "I don't even remember coming over here tonight." Then, suddenly, she grabbed her stomach and laid back down, her body retching in dry heaves.

"Oh my God!" Nonny screamed. "Mary, help her!"

Me? What was I supposed to do? Think fast; that's what I needed to do.

"Mandy, hand Amethyst to Nonny. Can you hold them both in those bulky towels?"

"Yes! Here, Mandy, let me have her. Help! Oh, my gosh! Oh, my gosh!" Nonny was upset.

Jade finally stopped retching on the floor.

"Get me an ice pack," I ordered Mandy after she'd handed the baby to Nonny.

"An ice pack for a vampire?" Mandy questioned.

"Well, I don't know. Do you have any better ideas?"

Mandy's eyes were enormous, and she got the ice pack from the freezer after all and then handed it to me.

"Here." Mandy kneeled with me. "Jade, it's Mandy." I put the ice pack behind Jade's neck after pushing her onto her back.

Jade looked at her, but it appeared as if no one was home. Mandy looked at me. "I'm scared, and of all nights, the boys are out. Maybe they would know what is going on and what to do."

"We'll have to make do until they get back. Can you help me lift her? We can lay her on the couch at least." Mandy nodded, and Jade stood as we helped her. For a vampire, she sure looked terrible.

"Maybe she has been gone too long from the Shadow Night," Nonny suggested.

"Perhaps," I told Nonny.

"Or maybe she's changing again?" Nonny questioned.

I nodded. "Perhaps."

"Maybe…" Nonny repeated something.

"Nonny dear, can you hold up a minute with your talking until we get Jade situated?" I said, a bit agitated.

This time Nonny nodded and went to the reclining rocker and sat down with the babies. Jet immediately started trying to nurse. "Good heavens," Nonny mumbled, and got him situated. Well, she was tied down for the moment. Maybe I could think!

Jade got to the couch in a dazed state and laid down quietly. I put the ice back on her neck. She removed it and put it on her stomach.

"No… no way." I shook my head in disbelief, knowing now exactly what had happened. She had been blessed. The baby would be here within the next month.

Chapter Three

Jade

Everyone looked at me like I was an alien or a piece of fine china. "I'm fine. Really. I can handle traveling back to the Shadow Night." I stood outside Tristan's Jeep, and all gazes were on me. "A few dry heaves here and there. A drop to the ground, maybe." I raised my finger as Tristan opened his mouth to say something. "I won't get up, move, walk, run, or anything without you next to me." He shut his mouth and then must have had second thoughts.

"We have to travel quickly, Jade. But I won't risk anyone's health here. We'll stop as needed, at morgues, and wherever else is required. We have a month, right, Mom?" Tristan asked Mary the same question for the hundredth time now.

Rolling my eyes, I pointed out, "It's four thousand miles. We'll stop as needed. I'll be fine." Then, looking at Mary, I asked her, "Please tell Tristan I'll be fine with you here."

Mary's eyes shifted a bit. "You should be fine, Jade, as long as we get you under the protection of the Shadow Night before you go into labor. I don't want to mislead you or anyone that this is safe, Jade. It's not."

"See?" Tristan sounded vindicated.

"However," Mary continued, "like you told Grant when Nonny was in labor, women have babies every day. In your case, though, we have the first royal baby in centuries, and the timing and how it happened with you is quite concerning. I'll feel much better having you protected by the realm of your people and not just us, but as far as your health, Jade, you're just fine."

"Okay. Well, that wasn't exactly what I was expecting to hear from you after you've been telling us all how fine things are." Irritated, I turned and lifted myself into the Jeep. I was done talking, and I wanted to be left alone. I slammed my door. Through the rear-view mirrors, I watched everyone else load the babies into Grant's Hummer. There wasn't a lot of room left in either Tristan's or Grant's vehicle, so Mary had traded in her car for something that would be better for the trip, a Range Rover.

With Buddy panting happily in the back of our Jeep, we were loaded and ready to convoy the drive out of Peebles, Ohio. The plan was to stay in the States to the west coast. There were plenty of morgues to stop at, as we had decided to stick to the roads, and when the vamps went to feed, Mary and Mandy could address whatever Nonny and the babies needed elsewhere. Our only hang-up would be Mary and Mandy needing to stop for rest. One would drive while the other slept for as long as that worked. Either way, the drive would take time.

Our first two stops at morgues to feed went reasonably well, considering I pretended like I was okay and not pregnant. I just finished a rapid dry-heaving session when we pulled into Salt Lake City, UT.

"Let me splash some water on my face before we go to the morgue, Tristan. Can you go to a gas station or something?" I felt like crap.

"Of course, sweetie." Concern in Tristan's voice spilled out. "I need to fuel up anyway, and I'm sure the rest of the caravan is ready to, as well."

Over two full days in a car with him looking at me like I was going to break had me more than on edge. The babies did better on the drive than I had, that was for certain. We stopped about every two hours for Nonny to nurse and change the diaper of one and someone else to bottle feed and change the other.

"I'll come around and help you. Just let me park and get to you from the outside." Although I agreed to Tristan helping me, this was getting old.

"Can you just give me five minutes of peace?" I yelled at him.

Stunned, he sat with his hand still on the key, as he turned the ignition off to hurry and help me get out. Buddy whined in the backseat.

"Sure, Jade. Just as soon as I get your ass to the bathroom! Take all the time you need. We have all day! All year! No pressure! Damn!" Getting out, he slammed thc door. Mandy came running over to my side of the car.

Opening the door so she could talk to me, she murmured, "Everything okay?"

"Fine. Just get me to the bathroom, can you?" I fumed.

"Sure, Jade. Umm, you want me to take your arm or what?" Mandy tried to be cautious. She didn't want to spike my temper anymore, but it was a little late for that.

"I don't know!" I yelled at her. I'd been trying to get out of the car, and when our gazes met, she backed away and ran back to Grant's car, where Tristan and Grant were standing together, filling up Grant's Hummer. I watched the theatrics play out in seconds as Tristan sprinted back to me.

"Get in the car," he whispered harshly to me.

"No. I don't want to. I want to go in and...." Well, what did I want to go in and do? I could smell fresh blood all around me now. The vapors of the gas filling our tank were nothing compared to the pints of blood surrounding me. The jolt of energy I felt was unreal! Tristan stared at me. He attempted to block me from looking out and keep any curious onlookers from looking at me.

"You're not well right now, Jade. Get back in the car." Tristan demanded, using his body with some force and pushing me back into the Jeep.

"Your Jeep is full. Ready whenever you're. You got this, Tristan?" Grant spoke from behind Tristan.

"Shut up, Grant. I have business to do here." What the hell? I would not leave until I satisfied my desires!

"Yes, Grant. Just stay on my tail. Keep pressure on the door so she can't get out until I get the auto-door lock on, would you? Then We'll meet you at the funeral home furthest from town, near the tracks," Tristan replied, without looking away from me. "Hopefully, not before then."

"You think a window is going to keep me from what I want?" Sarcasm oozed from my lips.

"Jade." Mary stood at the side of the car.

"What, Mary? What can I do for you now? I'm busy if you can't tell. Be a good Oracle and tell these guys to move." I growled.

"Jade, shut up!" Tristan quietly grunted through clenched teeth.

"Grant, Tristan…" Mary pushed something between us. "Put this in her pocket. It's all I have available right here. But it should help." Grant grabbed it from her and shoved it into my front pocket. Tristan held me still. I was fired up! And then… I wasn't. It was like the sensation of rain falling on my head and down to my toes. I was washed with peace and then shoved all inside the Jeep.

Tristan got in and drove quickly out of the gas station and onto the road. I could feel his stare drill into my skull. We sat in near silence, but Buddy hadn't relieved himself. I felt like shit. I made a complete ass of myself.

"Sorry," I muttered to Tristan. He didn't respond, and I could see he was still furious.

One by one, our three cars pulled into the destination and parked side by side.

Finally, Tristan spoke to me. "You okay?" I nodded. Buddy whined loudly and barked. He needed out! Tristan opened his door. "Go on, Buddy. Stay close. Wait here a sec, Jade. Okay?" I nodded again.

Tristan went over to Grant's Hummer, where everyone else waited. Mary and Mandy would leave their car and take the Hummer elsewhere, while the three of us would go to the morgue.

I heard them talking.

"Man, we were so close to having the cops called, and that would've been a mess to take care of; we don't have time for that shit," Tristan spoke with irritation. "All those people were freaking out."

"Especially the guy right next to you!" Grant's voice was much more relaxed. "He planned to take us both on. Man! People and their stupid human thoughts."

"Okay, well, we need to get out of here. Jet is not happy," Nonny said through her window. Mandy sat in the back seat, trying to soothe the babies.

"Did you know she was going to turn psycho, Mary?" Grant asked in humor.

I didn't think it was funny at all and I'd certainly was fed up, so I opened my car door. Tristan quickly came over. "I told you to wait." His eyes were gentle.

"I think we all know I waited long enough, and I'm well overdue." I wanted to cry. I felt humiliated.

"Sure." Tristan planted a kiss on my forehead. "Grant, can you put some water and food out for Buddy before you come in?"

Grant kissed Nonny goodbye and pulled his head back out of the window. "Got it. You guys go ahead."

I felt off, and terrible, and humiliated, and still starving. But people were not on the menu anymore. Thank God! Feeling something deep down inside me, I put my hand over my stomach. "I feel it."

"It's not an 'it.'" Tristan whispered and pulled me close. "It's our tyro. Come on… Must be a girl because she is already taking after you." Tristan pulled me toward the entrance, with us both wearing smiles. A girl? Could it be?

* * *

There weren't anymore morgues between us and our destination off the Alaskan coast. We successfully completed five days of driving, and I was more than ready to be back at the palace, not for me, but because of Nonny and the babies.

On the last leg to the palace, the cars were stocked full of necessities for a baby or vampire. We were now resting out in the wilderness, and I felt extremely vulnerable. Uneasiness erupted throughout the group, and Nonny was beyond exhausted. Mary, Mandy, and Grant all helped as much as possible, but her mental frame of mind was frazzled!

The weather was mild so far, as spring began happily melting the winter away. So Nonny had one less thing at least to worry about on this long haul, as the babies would not freeze to death while we sat outside.

"I hate how quiet everything is out here." I sat next to Tristan on a blanket we set out away from the group. Nonny didn't trust me again, even though I had the help of Mary's essence crystal. I couldn't blame her. My agitation and need to feed were still there. The crystal helped me to keep my mind over matter. I wasn't certain if Mary could recharge the dang thing or what because the more time I had it, the more it lost its potency.

Tristan pulled me back against his chest, so I sat resting between his legs. We looked on as everyone talked and passed the babies around in their group. Buddy ran around the group in circles, happy to be out of the car.

"I know. I feel it too." Tristan searched my stomach for signs of life. "You said you could feel her?" That was presuming the sex, he stated, was right.

"Yeah, probably nothing you can feel yet, though." but according to Mary, I was bound to balloon out anytime, with only a few weeks to go.

"Tristan." I needed him to get Mary without making a scene.

"Hmm?" He continued to try to sense the life at my waistline. "I need Mary." His hands stopped. "I need her to energize the crystal or whatever she has to do. It's weakening, and that, I assure you, I can feel as well. So sooner rather than later, we have several humans." Tristan kissed the back of my head and stood up, leaving me without a word.

We were back far enough from the group that it took a little time for him to get there. I watched his sweet derriere sway back and forth. Yep, that was all mine.

"Hello, Jade." Caught completely off-guard, I whipped around, confused, and was even more shocked to find Kiryana kneeling next to me.

"Kiryana?" I knew it was her, but we were out in the middle of nowhere, and here she was.

"Yes, it's me."

"What are you doing here? And all alone?" This made little sense.

"Goodness, no. I'm not traveling alone. I have plenty of company." Then, turning back toward where she came from, she beckoned to someone.

"Jade! Kiryana? What the hell? Kiryana!?" Tristan was jogging up quickly with Mary close behind. He didn't want to leave Mary unprotected after seeing other vampires emerging from the trees.

“Grant, get your family together and in the Hummer, along with Mandy,” Tristan hollered over his shoulder. Grant was standing up and watching the scene unfold near me, not sure what he should do.

Mary hustled forward. “Should I go back?” You could see the question she shot at Tristan and the intimidation she felt cast through her eyes.

Kiryana answered for Tristan. “Marissa, our beloved Oracle. You’re safe with me, and with this clan I bring forward. It is a time of celebration to know more brothers and sisters have come forward to bask in the light of our Queen.”

Tristan and Mary, or Marissa, as Kiryana called her, were next to me, and Tristan helped me stand. Kiryana stood up as well, dusting off her knees.

“Just one moment, Drobny,” she instructed the small group moving toward us. They did as she asked and stood distant.

“We have humans with us, Kiryana,” Tristan growled at her.

“It’s fine. They are fine. The Drobny’s mean no harm. They want to be a part of the Shadow Night, given all that has been unveiled. I assure you; they are safe and will not harm Nonny and Mandy,” Kiryana said seriously.

“And the babies, Kiryana? The ones you would not protect?” Tristan said heatedly.

“Oh, posh!” She brushed the question off like she couldn’t believe he’d asked it. “I was wrong, so wrong. Of course, I have since learned that. But what’s done is done. They are royal, to a point. It will be up to the other Elders and myself, once we get the baby’s back, to figure them out.”

I wasn’t sure if the crystal’s energy was heavily drained or just me, but I needed something. Kiryana looked at me like she knew something was off with me.

“Where’s Marissa’s crystal?” she asked, as if she had already seen the bulge in the front of my jeans’ pocket.

“No, Kiryana.” Mary stepped out from behind Tristan and came over to me. “Have you forgotten that unless I have given something to you, you may not have it?”

Kiryana looked flustered but said, “Of course, what was I thinking? My apologies, Marissa.”

"Come, Jade." Mary gently pushed my arm in the direction she wanted me to go, "Tristan, I don't have to take it from her so that I'll be safe."

"Yes, keep her, and the future king or queen, safe," Kiryana stated.

I whipped around at her. "How did you know?"

"I'm an Elder. What do you mean, how did I know? It is plain to see Jade. Plain to see." I didn't like Kiryana's tone at all. Mary gently pushed me forward. "Come on, Jade, before it's too late." If I could've huffed and puffed, I would've!

* * *

Still fuming from the conversation with Kiryana, I sat mumbling to myself, and although I'm sure my mood showed otherwise, Tristan inquired, "You might as well speak up and get it off your chest, Jade. Did Mary get the essence crystal thingy working again?"

"Yes, it's working! I'm a little pissed-off, is all!"

"That's apparent." Tristan looked from the road to me and then into his rear-view mirror. "What I don't understand is why?"

"Well, let's see. First, Kiryana knows I'm pregnant, and I don't like that she knows. Second, I missed the whole meet and greet with all those Drobny things, and I should've been the first to meet them! I'm the damn lady in charge here! Third, Grant even told you he'd never seen those vampires, or whatever they are, at any of the morgues. Yet, you all go with it because Kiryana says it's okay! Fourth, now she is okay with the babies, and these entirely new vampire thingies are fine with everything? Tristan, I honestly don't get it, and even Mary agreed with me." I glared at Tristan, but wisely, he now kept looking at the road.

"Why do you call them thingies and whatever else you said?"

"Well, I don't know. I mean, yes, they are part of us. But that Grant doesn't even know them bothers me. I mean, doesn't he know everyone?" Now that I said the words, I wondered if that was a little preposterous.

"There are a lot of vampires, Jade, and we are all moving around and changing things up. Changing names and appearances is a widespread practice. As long as we all live by the same laws, we don't know everyone personally. We all have our own lives to live, just like humans. Over the centuries, perhaps we have lost touch with how everything flows in the world of vampires. The Elders know this. It's not widely discussed because it causes fear about the system we have and live by; who wants that? Having you back is one step in a massive project of re-establishing the entire Shadow Night. All the Drobny are doing is confirming what the Shadow Night Elders have feared that there may be others. Who knows how long ago they stepped out or the reasons for it? They seem legit, Jade. We want this to happen because it protects you! I'm trying to keep you safe, that's all."

"Okay, but you said they seem legit, and I haven't met them, and I don't feel right about them or Kiryana," I said, throwing caution to the wind.

"I don't know how we all were at the same location. But much bigger things have happened without an answer. We move all the time, you know. At least we know they are out there and tailing us or ahead of us wherever. The point is, we are all going to the palace where it can all get pieced out and resolved." He paused, and I said nothing else.

"I hear you, Jade. However, I also have to trust Kiryana as an Elder. I'm sure Mary just agreed with you, not listening. She was trying to handle your other issues."

"Issues? The little one is an issue now?"

"Jade, quit making something out of nothing. Our tyro could cause a lot more havoc if Mary wasn't helping keep her in check. I think you're reading a lot more into it that isn't there because your body is changing again, and we all know how you're when your body is changing." Tristan tried to make light of the situation, but all it did was piss me off more.

"Just don't talk to me right now, Tristan. You're making me sick." With that, I began my not so blissfully dry heaving. The palace couldn't come into view soon enough

Chapter Four

Mary

Several members of the Drobny Clan strolled into one of the main palace rooms where I'd been sitting by myself. I smiled at them warmly, and they returned my greeting with a nod. They looked pretty bored to be there. The three of them sat across from me on the opposite side of the large resource room. The room felt heavy with them present, and I had a tough time collecting my thoughts. We all arrived together four days earlier, at the pearly white gates of the Shadow Night. It was far from a welcoming committee as we walked through the doors. I say all, but actually, Kiryana had been sent a little ahead of the group. We didn't want another battle on our hands. When new vampires come around, it makes the palace uptight.

It was a sight when we all approached. What was most unsettling was them not knowing Jade's condition. The announcement was met with cheers as we took another step forward in securing our place and the future of our race. Jade was whisked away for safekeeping, and a good vampire doctor's supervision had been started immediately. I hadn't seen her since.

Grant, Nonny, and the babies were taken in for their examination. From what I heard, there were fundamental questions, as they didn't pose a threat to anyone and were safely tucked away also, just as Jade had been, until the matter of this unknown Drobny Clan could be resolved. The Shadow Night learned its lesson of holding your friends close and your enemies closer. I knew soldiers were not far away, watching the three in the room with me. The Elders kept this clan in constant questioning, with Kiryana's support, the entire way.

Kiryana explained that she came across the Drobny Clan on her way back from the aborted binding ceremony of the twins. She had her hand slapped for failing to inform the other Elders of what was going on outside of the Shadow Night with its members and keeping this newly discovered clan a secret. Her defense was that this was only for the safety of us all. After all, she was a leading member of the Elders, and they should not question her choice of action when safety was involved, considering all that had happened to those of Shadow Night. It was her life she'd risked, not theirs. Once she felt secure with the new clan and trusted them, she intended to introduce them quietly because she didn't want to cause feelings of insecurity to other vampires within the clan. Then, she could turn the tables back on the Shadow Night for ruining all that and on me.

Because of Kiryana, I was looked at in a new light here at the Shadow Night. I was best known as Marissa, the Oracle, from a time of hardship and pain. They could not understand my state here and now, and they resented me for my involvement in past events. Many said I had betrayed them in every way possible, and it made me question myself. If they all thought I had, maybe I was the one in the wrong. I kept my mouth shut, offering no explanation, even though they demanded one. All I could tell them was that I thought what I was doing with the babies had been the right thing to do. I knew I had the support of the smoke people, which the Shadow Night didn't know about; so, I couldn't use them to justify my actions. I was caught between a rock and a hard place.

The air was too thick in here. I had been cut off from everyone and everything I loved. Even Mandy had been taken back to the continental states immediately. She was alone. I felt unable to help her and was ashamed that I had let all this happen. I had responsibility for all this. Yes, I did. Everything was changing, and I felt like I was the only one seeing it.

I had seen Grant one time and, if he saw me, he didn't acknowledge me. It broke my heart. I had to get out of here, out of this place. I needed my book and to figure out all this mess.

Standing up, I hustled out of the room with all three sets of eyes, sending stares that drilled through my back as I left. My room was my salvation. At least they'd given me my old room back. Stepping into it was like a breath of fresh air every time. I was welcomed, and it invited me in. So many memories filled my mind. Pain with peace. Tears with joy. My prior lives had all been completely unlocked. Time was moving on.

I sat on my bed, holding the large leather-bound ritual book. Flipping the pages slowly, I read and examined every pen stroke, looking for something I'd missed that could help.

"Marissa!" There was a loud knocking on my door. "Marissa, are you in there?" I didn't recognize the voice. It was a Shadow Night woman who had only known me as the Oracle, that much I knew.

"Yes." I closed the book and hurried off my bed to open the door. "What is it? What's wrong?"

Panic could be seen on the lovely vampire's face. "Jade, she's calling for you. The new royal tyro is near."

"What?" It was too soon, wasn't it? "It's too soon. Are you sure?" I questioned the woman with my thoughts. Finally, she shrugged and pleaded, "Hurry!"

"It's only been about ten days since we've known." I hurried after the woman. "We still have at least two more weeks! This can't be right!" We ran down the hallways to Jade and Tristan's suite. The door was shut, but I heard Jade on the other side.

"Where's Mary? Oh, God! Where is Mary?" she cried out.

Bursting into the room, I ran to Jade's side. "I'm here, Jade." I reached down, putting my cheek next to her wet, tear-stained face. "I'm right here. Calm down. Shh."

"I've been telling her to keep calm, but she wanted you." Tristan was at her other side. He sounded pretty bleak.

"Well, I'm here now." I looked Jade over, finally seeing her belly. "My goodness, Jade." I have never seen a tyro develop so quickly. Jade was still small, but she now looked like she had a completely different body in the several days since I had last seen her. "You sure keep us on our toes."

Looking at Tristan, I acknowledged him, finally. “Where are her doctors, and why aren’t they helping her?”

Sheepishly Tristan replied, “Jade hasn’t let one of them touch her or be near her since their initial exam.”

“Why did you wait so long to let me help?” I knew the answer already. I wasn’t wanted here now, as it was. “Shame on you and Grant for being so quick to judge. You two, of all people, should know better. Grant’s my blood! My grandbabies.” Jade interrupted my slap at Tristan with cries wrung from her because of a contraction.

“Mary, please help me!” Jade was in so much pain.

“I am here, Jade. And I’ll help you. Remember everything we did for Nonny and all the pain she had. It’s your turn, now.” I looked at Tristan for reassurance.

After checking Jade to figure out the baby’s position and how far she was dilated, I could collect my thoughts.

“She is only two centimeters,” I explained to Tristan and the other women who were in the room. “She has to get to ten.”

“So, how long?” Tristan demanded. Jade’s contractions were steady and long, but I knew labor was unpredictable.

“I’m not sure, Tristan.”

“Well, can’t you help ease her pain or anything? You’re the Oracle, and you’re back within the walls of the Shadow Night.” I didn’t like his tone. He hadn’t listened to a word I had said to him moments ago.

“Does she still have my essence crystal?” I asked him.

He shook his head, “No. They took it.” He implied my negligence again.

“Then no. I probably can’t help ease the pain unless you find it.” Tristan looked at one of the other women in the room. “Go see if you can track down Marissa’s crystal.”

After the woman left to do his bidding, I questioned Tristan. “You know, or I suppose, perhaps you don’t,” I answered his perplexed look. “Jade should not be in labor yet. There’s so much going on here, Tristan. No one can keep track of any of it. The Drobny, Nonny, and the babies. How are they, Tristan?”

He looked at me, perhaps not knowing what to answer first. “Why are you like this?”

He surprised me with his answer. “I have to. I’m sorry, Mary… Marissa. When there are….” His explanation was cut short as all the Elders entered the room, including Kiryana.

Tristan bolted up. “Seriously? You all barge in here without knocking?” Tristan ran his hand through his hair, upset. “This is like a damn circus.”

“She is bearing the new Royal Tyro. We have every right to be a part of this,” an Elder replied.

Jade cried out in pain. “Get out!”

“Please, let her labor in peace,” Tristan coaxed.

“Why is she in here?” Kiryana pointed at me.

“Because she is the only one Jade will let touch her,” Tristan said in my defense. “So, if you want a safe Royal delivery,” Tristan pointed to me. “She is going to have to do it.”

“Then We’ll stay.”

“It’s coming!” Jade screamed as her body did what nature asked it to do, and she pushed, screaming at the same time.

“Stay back, then!” I hollered over Jade’s pushing. “Tristan, help me position her.” I rechecked her and could see that Jade wasn’t wasting any time. This tyro was coming and coming like the speed of light.

“I need the suction, clamps, scissors, and gloves; I need clean gloves.” The woman who had left to find the crystal was back. She set the crystal on Jade’s bedside table and got to work doing as I asked this time.

Jade delivered the precious little tyro with her next push. A baby girl, screaming at the top of her set of pipes, letting the world know that she was here. Somehow, over those screams, I heard the bells sounding outside, that a new life had been graced among the vampire life. Nor was it just any life, but life from their king and queen. I felt the flush of emotion wash over me.

“You did it, Jade.” I was so elated with joy.

She was hugging Tristan, and they were both crying.

"Tristan, come cut the cord." The baby had calmed down after I finished suctioning her mouth and nose. But with the clamps on the umbilical cord, she was ready to be separated from her mother.

I looked back and saw all the Elders staring in awe. I had done my best to keep Jade from being too exposed during the delivery. I hoped they had the decency to give her that privacy as well. Movement at the back of the room, where the door had been partially opened, caught my eyes. Drobny eyes peered back at me.

"Right here?" Tristan touched my arm, wanting an answer.

Looking back at the baby, I realized Tristan was struggling with where to cut the cord.

"Hurry," Jade said, sounding exhausted, as she should've been. Labor had been most intense. "I want to see her."

"Hand me some clean blankets, so I can wipe her off a little and get her warm," I told the woman who was waiting nearby.

"What time was she born?" I asked the room.

"Six o'clock on the dot," an Elder answered. "The first of May, at 6:00 p.m."

"May Day," I said, not sure if the Elders would know what May Day was.

I handed the peaceful baby girl to Tristan to carry to Jade. "She is perfect," I told him. He smiled back warmly for once.

"Thank you, Mary."

"Hurry, Tristan," Jade whined. Tristan's gaze connected with his soulmates as he brought their little girl to her.

"Look, Jade. She looks like you," Tristan said proudly.

"Congratulations to both of you," I told them, and I meant it.

"Thank you, Mary, for coming for us." Jade snuggled her daughter close.

"Wouldn't miss it for the world," I told them.

The Elders had moved forward. "We can take it from here, Marissa, and We'll let you know if anything else is required from you." Well, that was a friendly slap to the face.

"Yes, I'm sure you will," I said, probably a bit too coy. I gave Jade and the baby a kiss goodbye. My essence crystal was still on her nightstand, so I discreetly picked it up as I walked away.

"Anything you need, Jade," I spoke to her as I backed away.

"I will," she said as I felt a hand pull me away.

Turning, I shook the icy hand away. "I'm going. I don't need an escort."

The door had been closed again, but I knew the being who had peered around it wasn't far away. It made me wonder how I could be ousted, and they could be allowed in.

I left the room, not even knowing the new princess's name.

* * *

Back in my room, I sat on my bed, focusing on the book, looking for answers to any or all of the questions I had. I felt like I was being held hostage in a place that I had saved. None of this was making sense. Jade and Tristan were supposed to come back to rule, and life was supposed to have gone on like any other story with a happily ever after ending.

Was it because the Higher Powers had returned me to being human after taking me away from here? What did they expect? Slamming the enormous book closed and lying on my back, I looked above me to the ceiling, the stars, the heavens; I could see it all in my mind, through my mind. I saw things that no one here could ever comprehend. Where was the judgment on them? The essence crystal rolled into my side softly.

"Why?" I raised my fist above me. "Why? Because I question you?"

"Mary?" Tristan was knocking softly at my door. "Mary, let me in before anyone comes."

Spinning back over, I cried, "Yes! I'm here. Quickly, come in." Then, sitting up and smoothing my hair down, I watched Tristan stride across the room quickly, looking determined.

"Sit." I patted the bed.

"How are Jade and the baby?" I asked him.

“Great. Everyone is doing great. I want to talk to you about everything else you asked in the room. Quickly though, I have little time, so I’ll cover it in pretty general terms.

I grabbed his arm. “First, I have to know. What’s her name?”

Tristan’s face softened. “Micah. Her name is Micah.”

“Like God.” It was a mighty name, and the meaning was perfect. Tristan nodded. “Boy or girl. That was the name chosen.”

“And it is a perfect name.” We agreed.

Tristan’s face changed back to the sternness he had when he entered my room. “First off, Grant, Nonny, and the babies are all thriving and doing great. Jade is sorry Nonny missed the birth, but Nonny is in with Jade now. That’s why I could get away.”

I nodded and smiled, waiting for him to continue, given his limited time. “As far as Jade and the pregnancy, and its short duration, the Elders are so far just attributing it to Jade’s new life here, and perhaps it’s how all her pregnancies, if there are more, will go. They have nothing to base it off, and they are clueless about how it happened so quickly. So they leave that blessing to the Higher Powers. They don’t know what else to think. It takes their intervention to complete the ritual once it has been offered, as you know.” Tristan rubbed his face in thought. “What do you think?”

“I’m not sure either. It’s difficult to understand, though, considering the history of the Shadow Night.” I put my palms up and shrugged. “What about the Drobny? I see them around everywhere like it’s no big deal. I don’t get it. This is a palace. A version of Fort Knox. Jade and a new tyro. Why aren’t the Drobny being housed away from here?”

“Kiryana.” Tristan shook his head. “She has everything the way she wants it. But, honestly, Mary, in their defense, they seem fine. If we can’t trust our Elders….” He let the sentence trail off.

“You’re sure? You’re not just saying that?” The Drobny face poking into Jade’s delivery room earlier made me feel otherwise.

“Yes. I have spent several hours downstairs in the lockdown room with all of them and the Elders. Unfortunately, Jade couldn’t be a part of it, but we introduced them to her before today at her request. They are all hitting it off very well. Jade has spent some time with a Drobny woman named Zoe. She is like their healer or medicine provider-type or whatever you want to call it. She has given Jade some great cocktails that have helped with the dry heaving. That was enough to make Jade think the Drobny female walked on water, believe me."

Why would they need a healer or medicine person? That made little sense to me. All the Shadow Night had doctor-types just for the tyros. What else was needed? I didn't question it. There had to be more to the story that he just didn't have time to tell.

"Mary." Tristan looked at me squarely. "They're getting ready to review what they think you have done."

Taking a deep breath, I exhaled slowly. "I know. I'm not afraid. I'm Marissa, Tristan. I'm a devoted member of this clan in any form. Anything I've done, I have done because I thought it was best and the right thing to do." A tear escaped.

Tristan stood, "I have to go. And I want you to know that as the King here, and Jade as the Queen, you're protected, no matter what the Elders say. You, as well as they, protected us, and I'll not let them forget." Tristan turned and got to the door before turning around.

Trust the Elders, trust the Drobny, and trust yourself. We are in some type of upheaval, but I just can't, for the life of me, think that the Higher Powers brought us this far for nothing. Tristan left, quietly shutting the door.

Well, he was right about one thing. We hadn't been brought here for nothing. I would trust myself, and somehow, I would get back to being the Marissa these vampires knew. My grandbabies were here, and I would protect them alongside Buddy. There's a purpose for everything. That I know! But the Drobny?? I couldn't see the necessity of them being here. That Jade had been drinking something given to her by them and that no one knew where this blessed tyro came from, and then the birth being weeks earlier than it should be, was all concerning. There was an explanation, but I would not sit around and wait for it when the damnation stepped in. Too much of a good thing. Well, that can't be good.

I deemed myself the Guardian of the Children and Oracle of the Shadow Night. Grabbing my essence crystal, I held on tight!

Chapter Five

Mary

It was bound to happen. I just didn't expect it to be here at the Shadow Night, of all places. I figured my youth would shine through, but what I saw in the mirror were crow's feet.

After five years of living back here at the Shadow Night, it was another thing I could add to my lengthy list of the unexplainable. They were subtle, but I could see them. Sticking my tongue out at myself, I left my bathroom and room. There were now two vast libraries here, and I searched the old one for clues that Jade's family may have left. Their ritual books had been destroyed, for sure, and new ones were being written, but it was a slow process to remember and create something so extraordinary in their place. The old library had thousands of books in it, and many had been partially destroyed. That room was almost the only room not to have been redone since the slaughter of Keegan's rampage. Restoring the room and items would've caused more loss than help.

Arriving at the door, I dug in my pants pocket for the key, as I wasn't supposed to be in this room. I always used caution when coming to and from here during my stay at the palace these past years. My role was no better than that of a wallflower here at the palace. I was the grandmother of Jet and Amethyst--who mainly was called Amy for short, after a person who had a history of having once been a great Oracle whom they felt had been stripped of her wings. Pretty harsh for someone who'd kept them alive for so long. Yes, my list was long with unexplainable things. But, I didn't mind the peace for now as I didn't want them to be aware of how insane the Elders were to think that I could be anything less than who I was. I had aged, but my powers had grown stronger.

I was thankful for the key, which had remained in my room during my years of absence, and used it to let myself in. Then, just as I was almost getting the door shut, a soft knock from the other side caught me off-guard, and I jumped in surprise.

"You scared the dickens out of me, Rhyan." She was the only Drobny living here, since Jade had taken a particular liking to her. I couldn't say I felt the same. It wasn't personal; I felt that way about all of them. Grant told me I had become bitter with life and everyone in it since coming here. Relationships were strained all over the place, so I kept my distance. As long as I could check on the twins and how they grew up, nothing else mattered. I no longer had Buddy's help to protect them, as he had been sent back to live with Mandy, poor Mandy.

"Hello?" Rhyan said impatiently.

My head was the only part of my body on her side of the door. "Yes, what?" I sounded just as impatient.

"I want to know what you're doing. Let me come in." She pushed the door. So, I would've to back up.

"I have some things to do in here, and I was looking forward to doing them by myself." So I would not be bullied around.

"Yes, well, unless you want me to let everyone know you're stirring up spells and whatnot, you'd better let me in. I would hate to watch you have your hands slapped and perhaps lose the privilege of seeing your grandchildren." She smiled evilly at me.

Damn! I knew it. It was about time one of these things showed its true colors.

"I don't think you're allowed in here yourself. Are you?" I shot back at her in a hushed whisper.

"I'm free to roam. Now, open the door before I start something," Rhyan said wickedly.

"I'll just come back later. Move, so I can come out and lock the door." I tried to push her back, but her strength was too much, and she pushed me back into the room and entered like it was nothing.

"Who are you?" I demanded in a hushed whisper.

"Someone who has had it with you nosing around, looking and interfering where you shouldn't," she hissed back.

"Interfering in what? I'm barely given the nod around here by anyone. How could I interfere when I'm not involved with anything around here?"

"You've been working at overthrowing everything for five years. I can tell you; you need to leave. Now! There's nothing here for you. You're a transient, and you need to go back to your kind." Rhyan continued to hiss at me.

"My kind." I almost laughed. "There's no one else like me."

"You're a human. I see nothing more. I would've killed you long ago if I could've gotten away with it. Perhaps something from a better time still lingered in your veins then." She sniffed at me. "You stink. You revolt even the human race."

"Rhyan, you give me more reasons to stay." I stood tall, short, next to her, but I didn't want to cower down.

"Stay away from all the children. All of them, or else." She finished by licking her lips.

"You don't scare me, Rhyan, and you certainly don't know who you're threatening. I'll go straight to Tristan with this, and it is you who will go, not me."

"You do that. I dare you." She looked around. "Well, I guess the books can wait for eternity now. Be the tattletale. We'll see who stays and who goes."

Rhyan turned and left me precisely wondering precisely that; who would stay and who would go? Should I dare make a scene? I couldn't focus on the task I came in here to do, so, leaving the library and locking the door behind me, I went back to the only room I felt completely safe in.

After moving through what seemed like endless halls with eyes staring at me, I finally made it back to the door of my room. Safely inside, I locked it behind me and went to my fireplace, and sat in the chair before it. The fire didn't burn in it, but I rocked for a long time. I had tough decisions to make.

* * *

Rhyan confronted me again several days later when she figured out I would not talk to Tristan. I had prayed day in and day out for guidance and looked to the book for help. It felt like she was part of a a trap, and I was the lure. I needed the Shadow Night on my side, whether they cared to have me. Grant and Nonny lived in a completely separate wing of the palace, and it was after I had visited with Nonny and the children, Rhyan cornered me outside in one of the palace's many frozen yards. It was freezing, and my warm clothes only helped somewhat.

"I warned you to stay away from the children," she scolded me.

"They are my blood. Blood! My blood!" I threw back at her.

Her lips curled up, and she laughed. "Yes. Funny, isn't it?"

She threw me off-balance, and I didn't know how to respond.

"What's wrong? Cat got your tongue?" She laughed, but then became serious once more. "This isn't a game, and things are about to get real. So I'm not asking you anymore. I'm now telling you to leave."

"I can't. I won't." I begged. She had me at my knees when days ago I thought I had her at hers.

"If you don't… you'll have to live with what happens, and believe me when I tell you this, it will all go back on you."

"My grandchildren? Would you hurt children? Why?" I pleaded with her.

"I don't owe you an explanation. There's only one I care about…." She eyed me as if begging me to guess.

"Jet…" I whispered his name because the day he was born, I knew he belonged to someone else. Despite being his twin, Amy had kept some distance from him. She was always thrilled to see me and confide that Jet wasn't nice to her, but her mommy and daddy would brush her off. At the tender age of five, Amy knew better, and I asked only once for her to give me an example. She placed her hand over her heart and said, "Jet hurts me inside, Granny, inside of here. He pinches me. He hurts me when he's mad."

I sighed, looking at Rhyan. "All right, but let me do it on my terms." She may have expected more of a fight, but I would have to do my work elsewhere. I would fight, and I wouldn't give up. I had the Light on my side. I wouldn't have to hide my powers away from here.

"Let me see the children a few times more and let me wait out the harsh winter. Give me your word; you'll harm none of the children." I asked for the deal.

"Do not speak your tongue with anyone, and I won't have to," she stated, and then thought. "Better. Don't be up to no-good, either. Other Drobny are arriving. You'll be watched."

I nodded. The Shadow Night was in trouble.

Rhyan left me shaking, but not from the cold. I watched her walk back to the house. Her head was held high and her body poised. And now I hated her. She approached a figure with a hooded cape at the door, and they held a conversation. Who could it be? Another Drobny, as Rhyan said? There would be more. I hadn't moved, yet I was pulled to them like I was a part of their conversation. I couldn't hear their words, but I watched their mouths move. "Diamonté," the one with the covered head said. I moved my gaze from the mouth and saw the cursed word had been spoken by none other than Kiryana. With a quick inhale, I was back in my body at my distant spot, realizing the two figures were gone.

* * *

Pacing my room, I couldn't sit still. What should I do? Who would listen? What would I even say? "The children are all in danger, as is the Shadow Night, because of Jade's confidante, Rhyan, and an Elder of the Shadow Night?"

And what was with me being pulled into a conversation like that from a distance? That had never happened before, and I didn't even know if I could make something like that happen again right now if I wanted to. A knock on my door pulled me from the frantic mess in my head.

"Who is it?" I tried to keep my voice even.

"Grant." Thank goodness for small prayers. He must be the answer. "… and Kiryana is here now, too. Can we come in?" No!

"Uh. Yes. Just give me one moment." Then, looking around the room, I grabbed the leather-bound book and shoved it under my pillow. The crystal was on the desk, where I had been thinking of trying out new spells on it but hadn't had the nerve yet.

Opening the door, I smoothed out my shirt. "Yes, hello. You caught me by surprise. I rarely have visitors." Trying my best to smile and act normal, I couldn't look Kiryana in the eye.

"Can we sit, Mother?" Grant asked. I could sense the concern in his voice, and he hugged me as he walked past me to the hearth area, where there was a couch and my rocking chair.

"It's good to see you, Grant. Unfortunately, I don't get to see my family near often enough as I should," I remarked. Grant shrugged off my implication of wanting more time with them. Instead, he looked at Kiryana, apparently confused by my statement.

We all settled into place. I chose my rocking chair while they sat on opposite ends of the couch. I looked at them, waiting for one of them to speak about whatever was on their minds.

"Kiryana has brought it to the Shadow Night's attention that you're unhappy here. So I felt it my duty to come and see for myself. I know I have been gone from here a lot, with my duty to the Shadow Night most of these past few years, so I had to find out for myself. Do you miss being a part of the outside world? Are your daily visits with your grandchildren and daughter-in-law not enough?" Grant didn't sound pleased.

I was taken aback by the questions and statements about the family, as they weren't true.

Kiryana spoke up before I could think of what to say. "I told him how close we had become again and that you often speak candidly about your wishes of being back with your people, like Mandy and your dog. I couldn't let you continue being so unhappy here." Kiryana spoke softly and convincingly like she cared and as if we previoulsy had those conversations.

"So, before you think you're hurting my feelings or anyone else's, Kiryana and I have come up with a plan for you to go back to your 'home' so as not to hurt your grandchildren and Nonny." Ouch! I felt like Grant had hit me in the gut. I looked at Kiryana and saw her warning glare.

"And you say everyone knows about how I feel?" I directed the question to Kiryana.

"Yes, I blabbed everything. Finally, I couldn't hold it inside anymore. Even the sickness you say you've been having. I'm sure you need to visit your human doctor and get on something. Those thoughts are dark and unsafe. Perhaps the Higher Powers didn't think things through, using you in a way they probably shouldn't have." She paused. "I mean, we are all grateful for your love and dedication to us all so long ago." Kiryana stretched the words to make it seem like I was here at the beginning of time. Sure, it had been some time, but now my life was to be discarded in a lie. The Higher Powers would one day strike Kiryana down. Betrayal never won.

I had been cornered by lies. They all thought I wanted to go and was a loony bird.

"I can see it in your face, Mom. You aren't well. Would you like to hear the plan?" Grant's voice softened, and the look on Kiryana's face toughened.

Before answering, I looked out of my floor-to-ceiling windows. Words could not describe the beauty the place held. It would be a cross to bear if anything happened here in my absence like it had before. There would be no one to help this time, to carry on the legacy of Shadow Night. The innocent children would pay for the negligence. Jade and Tristan were running the palace. They reigned, as they should, in the clan's eyes; however, it was the Elders wagging the tail. I had to believe it wouldn't matter where I did my planning, as long as I had eyes on the inside. I knew what to do to get that, too.

"I'll desperately miss my family within these walls." Because I would! "I'm not feeling right; that is true." I couldn't confide in Grant all the lies that

Kiryana, and who knew who else, had planted within the walls about me. I wasn't sick at all because I was shielded by the Higher Powers as an Oracle forever. The only genuine statement was in my face. As it was changing, I was showing age.

"Whatever your plan is, I trust you. May I speak to you in private, Grant?" I wanted to appear fragile and willing. "It is only for the sake of the children that I did this. You know that."

"Of course, Mom." Grant looked relieved to get the hard part out of the way.

"I'm sure it doesn't matter whether I'm here or gone, Mary. You've spoken so openly with me for all these years, and I would love to help you in any way I can." Kiryana was set on keeping Grant on her side and staying.

"It's okay, Kiryana. It's been a long time since my mother, and I have spoken," Grant replied tenderly.

"As you wish, your Highness." At least Kiryana held him in some respect, as she should. Unfortunately, he was also a part of Diamonté. Curse that being!

Kiryana left, leaving the door wide open. "The door, Grant?" I asked quietly.

In a flash, he had closed the door and came back to his same spot. "What about the children?"

"I don't want them to forget me. They are young. May I give them something other than my time before I leave? I so want to know about their lives. Perhaps something I used to do daily is a habit they would take to?"

"I think that would be a great idea. It isn't like you're banished from here. I'll check in on you. Perhaps the children will too when they are older. For now, you know they cannot." I nodded, understanding what he was saying. "Nonny hasn't been excellent either. I worry about her being here as well." Grant said, deep in thought. "Unfortunately, I cannot give her the freedom to leave. I can you." I nodded again.

"One more thing, and I say this only because I don't want you to forget who I'm and what I once represented. Be on your mark, Grant." I warned him.

"Oh, Mom!" Grant chuckled. "Let your mind be at peace. All this new life and other new clans among us. It is simply amazing and should be embraced." His eyes suddenly looked sad. "Seriously, though, relax and do whatever you were doing before we all came into your life."

My warning fell on deaf ears. I couldn't force a smile. I couldn't force happiness where there would be sadness. "The smoke people live within, Grant. Don't forget."

"I never forget. Now, if you'll excuse me, I have to go check on my rambunctious kids and see what no-good antics they are up to." Grant stood up. "That Jet, he likes to play tricks. His mind is one nonstop working machine. I like to think he takes after me," saying it with pride.

"And Amy?" I asked.

"Is the most delicate flowering vampire that I have ever come across. Like the most amazing, calming breath of fresh air in the world. Perhaps she's like Nonny was when she was young." He became saddened, apparently thinking of Nonny and her state.

"Anyway, I'm glad we talked. This isn't a terrible thing, Mom. I want you to know we all want to see you happy and well again. Visiting is a must," he said, planting a kiss on my cheek. Before I knew it, he was out the door, which gave a soft click as it shut.

I fell back into my rocking chair and sobbed for what may have been hours.

I had little time to prepare to leave. It had to be time well spent. I needed several books from the old library, and if I couldn't find any journals that had unused paper in them to make new journals from, well, I would see about that first.

I went to my bed and pulled the leather book out from under my pillow. Tracing the letters as I walked to my desk, I set it down next to the essence crystal. It was time to play with magic. Who knew how long I would be kept away from Jet and Amy? I worried so much about the little ones, especially Jet. It wasn't his fault--his make-up and the curse of his ancestors.

Whatever I had done for their binding the night of their birth, I would do, repeatedly. Rhyan and the rest of her demon clan had a plan in the making, and I knew where it was coming from; Diamonté, and he wouldn't stop until he had his way, like a disease that wouldn't go away.

I had everything but the books from the old library. My desk had a retractable closing lid on it. After shutting it, I hurried off to the library, making sure I wasn't being followed. Quickly entering the room and closing the door, I breathed a sigh of relief, leaning my back against the door. "Shoot!" I said aloud. I forgot to lock my bedroom door.

"What's wrong?" Jade questioned me. I must have jumped about three feet off the floor in surprise.

"What are you doing in here, Jade? You almost gave me a heart attack." I said, grabbing my chest, feeling my heart slamming into my chest wall.

"Hi, Grandmamma." Micah was with her.

"Oh, child. Come, hug me already!" I bent my knees and opened my arms up to her. She came running in for a big hug. Then, lifting her little, light-body, I carried her over to where Jade was. She had several books laid out in front of her. An area with toys showed where Micah had been playing next to her.

Jade plopped back down into a chair, flipping the book over to read the front myself. "Dream casting?" She nodded, and I set Micah back down to play with her toys. "Can I help?" I asked Jade.

"I don't know." She looked at Micah. "I'm just not sure who…." Jade couldn't finish. I could see she was upset. "I'm so confused, Mary, and I have little time. Can we talk later?" she asked, motioning her head to Micah.

"Any time… although I suppose you know I'm leaving." Lowering my eyes, I was fearful about what I could say.

"Yes. And I understand. You'll be missed." Jade sounded sad as well.

"Later, then? Tonight? I don't want to wait." She again looked at Micah so that I would know for sure it was about her.

I would have to do the journals another night, but I could still get what I needed from the old library.

"Sure. That would be fine. I'm going just to grab a couple of books while I'm in here," I said as calmly as possible. It didn't matter anyway, as Jade had her head back down, reading her books.

"Okay." Her head popped up. "Can you take a few of these back with you? I don't want to be caught with them."

I didn't want to be caught with them, either. Who knew what I would get accused of before leaving? Suddenly, leaving the palace didn't sound so bad.

"You bet." Smiling at Micah and ruffling her hair, I went quickly to do my book search and get back to my room as soon as possible.

Chapter Six

Mary

I hadn't planned on starting anything until after Jade came and went. It was questionable whether she would show. She had a list of duties expected of her to do constantly. She may have already used up the only alone time allotted to her for the day by the Elders and other clan members.

"Lapse in time. Written in story rhyme, thoughts in crayon bound by no man. Take me with you, children, and let me see the magic unfold within thee." Not a terrible start for writing off the top of my mind. It needed lots of work, for sure, but the other items I needed, I had. That was a relief.

My stomach rumbled. I used to look forward to mealtimes, especially with Jade cooking. Now, the Shadow Night had stocked a good supply for us non-blood-drinkers. Unfortunately, it was all prepackaged and processed. Yuck. The grandbabies went for either blood or food, depending on their cravings. It would be awhile yet. I would think before they preferred nothing but the latter.

I had changed into my lounging clothes and slippers after returning from the library. I didn't want to change. If more Drobny were coming, and with this place not having a downtime because very few of slept, I changed back into my daily wear. I had let my hair grow as well, so I needed to do something with it quickly before I went down to the dining hall that had been erected for me back in the old days.

Brushing my hair and staring at my reflection, I still couldn't believe the changes that were slowly coming to my once fair, flawless face. Back in the day, I could've passed for a vampire. I hadn't been one, though, ever. Just your average Joe Oracle is what I would be to them now. I would eventually surprise them to save the day again. I hoped. There was more hair in my brush, I noticed, after finishing my ponytail. A little gray hurt no one. Well, a little, I reminded myself. With one last side-glance, I turned the light off and went in search of dinner.

Before making it into the kitchen, I realized the light was on and heard clattering coming from inside.

"Be calm, children." It was Nonny in there. I stood to the side, listening at the entrance. "What do you want? And don't tell me a cup of chocolate blood again, Jet. That may sound yummy to you, but to Mommy, it sounds gross."

"Can I have these, Mommy?" Amy asked sweetly.

"Yes, Amy. I wish your brother were as easy to please." Nonny said in a drained tone.

"Owie!" Amy cried out in pain. I had a feeling I knew where the pain was coming from.

"What's wrong with Grandmamma's big girl?" Amy squealed and ran over to me.

"Grandmamma." She leaped up into my arms and bear-hugged me. "What's wrong with the little miss?" I asked Amy, looking around her for Jet.

"It's gone, now Grandmamma. You always make everything better." My heart sank at her comment. I would have to tell them, but not tonight.

"Jet, come hug me. Grandmamma has missed seeing you, too." I reached out to him, trying to pull his sister off my neck.

"Go on and give Grandmamma a squeeze while I get you both your dinner." Nonny sounded grateful for the interruption.

"How are you, Nonny?" I gave Jet just as big a bear-hug with my free arm as his sister had given me. Amy wouldn't let go.

"Fine. Tired, I guess." Her back was to me. If she lost any more weight, she would be nothing more than a bag of bones.

"Honey, you don't look good." I wanted to be honest with her. "Can we sit and talk? Like old times." Referencing to living in Peebles.

"Yeah, sure, I guess. Let me heat these cans for the kids." Nonny hurried along so we could talk.

"Come sit at the table, kids. Grandmamma is going to open a can of something or other and join you. Nonny? Can I help make something for you?"

"Not hungry," she replied.

"Humph! We are all going to sit down and have a family meal," I told the kids as they sat at the table, waiting to be served.

"We need Daddy here for it to be a family dinner," Jet said, sounding excited about the event.

"Here, Jet. Color with me, please?" Amy asked, giving him some paper and colored pencils that had been lying on the table already. "Draw me a castle that I can color in. With a prince and a horsey," Amy instructed Jet.

"Okay." Jet seemed to switch gears and grabbed a black pencil. He drew quickly and accurately, making it hard to believe that an actual adult artist hadn't drawn the picture for his sister to color.

"What else should I draw?" he asked Amy. Nonny came behind them and set their food down in front of each.

"Nothing, it's dinnertime," she told them.

"Goodness, Jet! Your drawing capeabilities! I mean, I knew you drew, but the last time I saw it, was nothing like this. Beautiful, Jet." He beamed at me.

"I like to draw," he said before shoveling in some ravioli.

"I can see that. Now, I'd better get something for your mom and me before you're done, all too quickly." I found a couple more canned meals and cranked them open.

"Sit, Nonny. It will be a moment," I told her, nodding for her to take a place at the table.

"Where is Grant this evening?" I asked, making small talk.

"Daddy left." Jet answered for his mom.

"That's why we're so late in the kitchen tonight." Nonny sounded sad.

"Oh. Work?" I asked.

"Always." Her tone was now quite dry. Both of the children quit eating and looked at their mother.

"How is dinner?" I asked, changing the subject. I got the feeling this was probably not a pleasant topic for the rest of the evening. I set Nonny's food in front of her and moved to a chair directly across from her.

"How about a play date with Grandmamma tomorrow?" If allowed, of course, I added to myself. I was hoping I would be given some extra freedom with them before I left.

Nonny looked at me with the first glimmer of hope I had seen in her eyes in months. "That would be so much fun. Can you?" She licked her lips in anticipation, and her eyes were wide.

"I think so. I believe a party is way overdue, don't you all think so?" I excitedly asked them.

"A party?" Amy asked. I nodded. "Oh, please! That would be fun." Amy got up and danced around the room like any other child might.

"What kind of party?" Jet sat thinking and watching his sister.

"Any kind of party," I told him. "What kind would you like?"

"A birthday party, with cake and ice cream?" he questioned, finally, some excitement out of the little guy.

"Sure!" I said. "It can be everyone's birthday tomorrow." Nothing like celebrating for all the ones to come that I would surely miss.

"Can I invite Pax?"

Amy came running back to the table, interrupting her brother. He scowled at her as she exclaimed, "Oh, no. I don't want him. Can it just be us, Grandmamma? Ouch!" she whimpered, holding her stomach.

"What's wrong, darling?" I asked, looking at Jet out of the corner of my eye. He was looking down, tracing the table with his finger.

"It's the food," Nonny explained to meme.

"What's wrong? Not enough of the other?" I quizzed them.

Amy crawled up into my lap. "Make it stop, Grandmamma." She snuggled in closer.

Kissing her forehead, I held her and spoke to Nonny. "And Jet?"

"He seems to be fine with whatever, or whenever. Of course, he prefers the other, but you know he has always been a good eater." She meekly smiled.

"The older Amy gets, the more problems she has. Of course, no one knows anything," Nonny relayed helplessly, holding her hand up in frustration. "I wish I could take her to my old pediatrician in Idaho. My parents beg me every time to bring them home." She looked away sadly, trying to hold back the tears. "I only get to talk to them once a month. The kids talk a little to them. But you know how that is."

When are they going to let you go visit? I wondered.

"As soon as these guys get old enough to handle their responsibility… to bend the truth." She made direct eye contact to make sure I understood; the reality of not discussing the vampire world with anyone.

I nodded, understanding. "Can't they do the mind-bend throughout visits?" I knew they could. I wondered why they wouldn't.

Amy pulled her food over to her so she could eat while sitting in my lap. Then we all took bites of our food, and I waited for Nonny to answer.

Whether she wouldn't or couldn't, I would not get my answer tonight.

"We should probably hustle up in here." Nonny pressed the children to eat faster.

"Tomorrow then?" she asked me as she collected dishes and took them to the sink.

"What about my Pax?" Jet asked me again. He was looking more at Amy than at me with his question.

I had to be fair, and perhaps it would be a wonderful learning opportunity to see a Drobny in action. I would keep Amy close. "Is he here?" I asked Jet.

"Yes," Jet stated, giving me no further details.

"Okay then." I squeezed Amy in reassurance.

"Anyone for you, little lady?" I asked her.

"No," she answered me sadly.

"Okay then. I'll get someone to give you the details. After that, I'll work on getting the festivities planned." Standing up, I hugged everyone goodbye.

"I hope to see you tomorrow, but I won't be surprised if something happens. It's okay." Again, Nonny looked away from me.

"We'll figure it out." Then, patting Nonny's arm, I wanted her to understand that I could read between the lines.

"It's tiring, putting on a show." Nonny relinquished the last sentence as she exited the kitchen.

"Well, that was interesting." I was by myself again. "Crap!" I jumped back out of the chair I had been sitting. I had forgotten about Jade! Practically running around corners and down halls, I plowed right into Tristan and Grant.

"Grant! I thought you were away, on duty?" I completely ignored Tristan, not meaning to but Grant?

"Nice to see you, too." Tristan laughed, slapping Grant on the back. "Come to headquarters when you're done here." He told him. "Got to run. Drobny are filtering in." He sounded excited about them being here. It made my skin crawl.

"Why are you so surprised to see me?" Grant looked amused.

"I ate in the kitchen with your family, and Nonny said you were gone." I was so confused and concerned. Soulmates should always know what is what. Something was not right here. Had she lied to me and not known? What? Why would she do that? That didn't seem like her.

Grant scowled. "Oh, well. Our communication has been a little off."

Communication? Off? "Are you guys fighting?" Placing my hand on his arm, I was genuinely concerned now.

"I don't know, Mom. Things are so off that I don't know what's right anymore." He confided in me, looking defeated, and it broke my heart. He ran his hand through his hair, almost nervously. "I can't talk to you about it right now. I have to go. Tristan and the rest are waiting."

"Grant?" Whirling around, I remembered I needed to talk to him about the party I was planning the next day.

Without even a hug or a goodbye, he was gone.

"What the heck?" I questioned aloud. Brushed off again, I trudged back to my room. If Jade came and left, I couldn't tell.

"What an evening." Leaning against the inside of my door and looking around the room, I didn't know what to do. Should I work on the twins' journals or go to bed? I sure wasn't tired anymore after all the events of the evening. So, journals, it was then.

"Okay, Mary. Let's get this done tonight because tomorrow at the party would be the perfect time to bring them each a gift." I knew nothing about Jet's little playmate. "They are all young still, Mary. Quit worrying so much. You bound them with some protection, and that has done something over these last few years." Relaxing into my desk chair, I opened the drawer that contained all the items I needed for the spell laid in there, in no particular fashion. If someone came in and looked through my stuff, the journals from the old library would catch their eye. But they wouldn't know what I was planning. I was sure of that. To them, I had become Mary over the years. Just… Mary. Even me being with Diamonté had gone to the back burner. Like the story of Sleeping Beauty with a spell cast over the kingdom to sleep. I wasn't sure that anything like that was happening here. But I couldn't rule it out either.

Pulling out several books and items from the drawer, I felt like the space wasn't big enough. So, I took each item over to the fur rug next to the fireplace one by one. If Jade showed, I would be exposed as being more than any of them thought I was, and I didn't want that. I needed to stick to the plan in place, but I also had to get these journals done.

A fire was definitely in order, and it would also set the mood to help me work. What I would make tonight for my grandchildren would not be easy. They would have to use them. That might be a problem or might not. Jet was a master at drawing. Could I make the pictures come through to me? Tapping a pencil against my forehead, I realized I didn't think it would be a problem. It would become a picture in my head, like a stamp. Amy's would become a movie in my mind. Whatever she wrote would be like I was there, and vice versa: pictures and writing. I groaned at the one thing I had forgotten. "They don't even know how to write yet. I hoped I could encourage Amy to draw her pictures rather than having her brother drawing in hers." Muttering, I continued to talk to myself.

"What if I made a journal for them to use each year of their lives? Well, that's all good and fine, but only if they use them." I answered my thoughts.

"Can I urge them with a spell? Should I urge them with a spell?" I was pretty confident I could muster up just about anything, with the way my Oracle powers were bubbling up in me. How could anyone not see it here in the palace? Whatever the reason, I was thankful for their blindness at this moment, which brought me back to the Sleeping Beauty question. "Was it me, or was it them, or was it all of us?" I didn't even remember standing up, but I paced. "Oh, the changes this place has seen. The original Royal Clan would be beside themselves." Striking a match, I lit the kindling in the fireplace. It was so mesmerizing, and then it happened.

The smoke danced around me like it was moving to the beat of a drum I couldn't hear. Up and down, side-to-side, it wasn't thick at all and smelled of strong tobacco. I breathed in deeply, welcoming the rich scent. It was about time the smoke people answered my prayers and brought me to them.

The vibrant colors of the Chief's costume coming toward me brought a smile to my face. For the first time in a long time, I felt safe. It was also the first time he'd come to me alone. I couldn't even make out a fire anywhere.

The old Chief stood before me, staring at me long enough to make me wonder if I was supposed to say something. Had I called this meeting, or had he? His eyes were very black and shiny, like a small, polished piece of coal, and they told me nothing. He jutted his jaw forward and then reached out and drew a line with his finger down the center of my face. When he was done, he motioned for me to follow him. I walked behind him, enveloped in his light tobacco smoke. I could see the dance of orange flames in the distance. We were heading to the fire circle, after all.

"Come. Sit." The Chief showed me where to sit on his right, but we were still alone.

"Did you bring me here, or did my heavy praying and light Oracle work bring me here?" I had to know.

He grunted back in reply.

"Please tell me this one thing without it going unanswered or obscured in a rhyme." My tone held a plea for a genuine answer.

He wouldn't look at me, just continued staring into the light of the fire. The fire snapped and crackled with the small flames that burned there. Again, we sat in silence for some time.

"It complicated." He still looked into the fire. I couldn't agree more, but which mess was he talking about?

He nodded. "Yes. Many." I forgot he knew what was going on in my mind. He chuckled ever so slightly. "Yes." He answered what I had thought.

"Tell me?" I asked out loud for the third time.

"Why it matter?" He took a long inhale from his tobacco pipe.

"It matters to me for future endeavors. I have a lot going on. A lot of complicated things going on." Touching on the severity of my statement. Everything had consequences in life, good or bad.

"I'm going to be leaving the palace and my grandchildren. While I have an idea to help me stay up to date on their current lifestyles, it would be nice to have some backup elsewhere, when it is just Mandy and myself."

"Hmm." He nodded. "Dog?"

"Is with Mandy. The palace wasn't a good place for him anyway, and Mandy would've been alone. So, I have had minimal contact with them."

"Hmm." He nodded again. "Your spirit, it grows?"

"Yes. Although no one has noticed it around me." I paused. "At least I think that is the case."

Finally, the Chief looked at me. "You're coveted for now. You take path of destination." He nodded. "They know," he said in his tribal dialect.

"Who knows?" Here we go, back to the rhyming.

"Dark people. Spirit no bright. You understand?" He inhaled another long hit from his pipe.

I was trying to stay calm, but I was tired of the riddles. Rising from the log, I stood before him. "Please! By the grace of God, can you speak to me directly?"

He looked up at me, unalarmed. "Through your weave, Oracle light is heard. Fear not what is destined before you," he replied calmly.

Throwing my hands in the air, I walked around to the other side of the circle. "Is there no mercy?" I asked, over the low flames almost dying out.

"Always there be mercy," he replied. "Find strength, Oracle one. Your hands are your glory. Your mind is a path. Your body a vessel." He stood now and pointed his pipe at me. "You no forget. Children." He shook his pipe at me again. "Your work has begun."

"Yes, the children." Coming back around the circle, I stood in front of him. "What of the children? Jet, he's so innocent, and yet he's so…" I couldn't think of the words.

"Powerful," the Chief said.

"Powerful? No, I wasn't thinking about that. But do you mean now or later? What is his destiny? Can you tell me?" My hands together, I waited in anticipation.

"His blood runs still?" he asked.

"Yes… yes, I believe so. Jet is still so young, but I feel so different toward him than I do for Amethyst." I confessed.

"As you should. But no how you think. Girl have path, as do boy. Reach to your bond, and do not be surprised." He ended.

The riddles would be my death. My hands went to my sides in frustration. Finally, I turned my back on him. "Please don't make me hurt anyone." Closing my eyes, I knew it wasn't the way of the Oracle ever to hurt anyone, especially my blood. But I had a feeling that if I missed something, any of their lives could be broken.

"A time of unravel. Binding be forced out. Be prepared. That is all I offer you." He came beside me again and handed me a small, closed pouch.

"What is in it?" I wanted to look for myself, but I held back.

"Something for work now. You no alone. Universe still unsettled." He wasn't done speaking, and so I waited.

"Spare none. Be precise. Where dark, find light. Where good, find evil. Battle continue… Jade only beginning," he said sadly.

"So, there have been more all along? And here we all thought Jade was the end?" He nodded his head.

Sighing deeply, I didn't know what else to say. I had plenty to ask still, but my questions would continue to be unanswered.

"Will you bring me here again?" Perhaps changing the way I asked a question would get my answer.

"Yes." His tone was relatively quiet for him.

"Universe will settle?" I wondered.

He looked at me, "Always."

"Soon?" I asked, wondering what the timeline might be.

He shook his head. "Hard travel. Quests… no written. No done yet. Patience, Oracle one."

"Patience." I nodded. "Working on that. But these vampires and children scare the life out of me. I'm aging. Can you see?"

"Hmm." He nodded. "Fear not."

I wanted to wrap up our conversation to make sure I understood, but he put his fingers over my mouth to keep me from speaking.

He removed his hand and placed it over the pouch. "Here." Then he moved his hand to my head. "Here." And then took it down to my heart. "Here."

Again, he took a long hit from his tobacco pipe and blew it into my face.

The smoke cleared quickly after that and became smoke coming from the direction of the fireplace.

My hand still gripped the pouch securely. I was thankful that I still had it with me. It made me feel safer knowing they were not far away. I had to work on my patience with them, for sure. I had to trust myself and the knowledge that these Higher Powers placed on me. I was one of them still. I had to believe.

Everything was still as I had left it. The books and items were untouched on the fur rug. I set the pouch on the fur as well.

A knock on my door startled me. "Yes?" I answered, looking over at the door.

"It is Kiryana. You need to let me in. Now," she demanded quietly.

She wasn't someone I wanted to see at all right now! "This isn't a good time for me." I had to think fast. "I just got out of the shower. Can I meet you somewhere, tomorrow perhaps? It's late, and I need my rest."

I could see the knob trying to turn, and I could not have her in my room. The door was locked, but who knew what she could do. I didn't trust who she was anymore.

"It's locked, Kiryana. Take your leave, and I'll come to you in the morning," I told her as I came across my bedroom floor. I surely would be no match to keep a door closed against her. Everything was out, including the pouch. I could feel the adrenaline kicking into my body.

When I got to the door, I noticed a piece of paper had been slipped under it. There were now two voices in conversation on the other side. Unfortunately, the voices were low, so I couldn't hear who the other one was. Reaching down, I quietly picked up the paper and then held my ear to the door, attempting to listen in on the conversation. My heart was thudding against my chest like a drum. I was sure the vampires heard it clearly on the other side of the palace.

Finally, I heard footsteps walking away from my door, but I couldn't tell if it was one or two sets. I waited at the door in fear. If Kiryana was still there, she didn't speak. My mind told me she was still there and, like a scared cat, the hair on my neck still stood up in fear.

"Please go away," I spoke through the door. There was no reply nor sound of footsteps leaving. I again heard the Chief tell me in my head to ''fear not.' I had to believe in myself!

I stepped back from the door and tucked the note into my pants pocket. Then, closing my eyes, I knew it was time to try a little something.

Raising my hands toward the door, I whispered what came to mind. "Bound by light, cursed by dark, on your honor, you left your mark. Bound by spirit, born to light, distance them from me now tonight. Hear my prayer, hear my chant, in this room, I stand in High Powers' light. Hallowed vampires near and far shall never enter this chamber hall."

Footsteps ran from my door. Mission accomplished! I felt completely depleted of energy, and an area of my head felt hot. I felt my hair where the sensation was emanating. It even felt hot to the touch. I had to see what was going on, so I headed for the bathroom.

I was shocked at what I saw in the mirror when I flipped the light switch on. "Oh, no!" There was a dark line down the center of my face and a streak of white down my light brown hair! I was thankful more than ever that my door hadn't opened. The line down my face would've been something I couldn't explain. God only knows what Kiryana would've done to me or what her plans had been from the beginning! Now, should I worry about what had happened to my hair?

I could tuck my hair into a hat tomorrow, which would solve that problem. Then, turning on the water, I grabbed a washcloth and tried to scrub the black line away. It took a lot of soap and hot water, but it faded, and all I was left with was a red line down my face.

"Hope you go away by morning," I told the line in the mirror.

The clock was ticking to get the journals done on time, and I hadn't even seen what was in the pouch.

"The note!" I had almost forgotten as I pulled it from my pocket.

Mary,

I couldn't get away this evening as I had hoped. I had forgotten more of the Drobny clansmen were coming.

I need to see you as soon as possible. I'll figure out somehow a way to let you know when. Please keep this all silent.

Also, if you make it to the old library again, I have left a few books near where you were today. They are at eye level on the end, slightly uneven from the rest.

Please destroy this message. All I can tell you is how I feel right now, and I feel unsafe and confused.

Sincerely,

Jade

P.S. I heard you were having a party in Nonny's wing. I'm hoping to have Micah there.

Chapter Seven

Mary

At my arrival, Amy ran over and squealed, “Grandmamma!” Micah jumped up and came barreling over to me for a hug as well.

“How are my two favorite girls today?” I asked them both as I bent down and hugged them. I had the journals wrapped up in paper, so it was a little awkward. “Here. Let Grandmamma put these presents down so I can give you giant bear-hug squeezes.”

The girls both giggled and stepped away so I could set the gifts on a counter nearby.

Amy clapped her hands together. “You brought presents? For me?”

“For you, Micah, and Jet,” I eagerly replied. The spell had worked beautifully, and I didn’t doubt that the pouch containing various colored war paints from the Native American Chief was responsible. I made the journals as fat as possible since I didn’t want to miss a thing! All I had to do was make sure each child traced the front cover design of their appropriate journals with a finger. That would set the need to write and draw in motion. Their emotions would be recorded in their respective journals during their times of need to figure things out. Whatever angered and stirred Jet to be different would show. Whatever pain, trouble, or joy Amy felt, she would write it down.

"How did you know I would be here?" Micah asked with interest.

"A little bird told me." I touched her nose. Her beauty was mesmerizing, and the Higher Powers guarded her soul. I had used extreme caution making her journal. If her things were ever looked over, I didn't want there to be a question that led someone to come looking at Jet and Amy's journals.

"Where is Jet?" I asked Nonny as she finally came over to greet me.

"He's playing in his room with a friend," she told me in a drained voice.

"Oh yes, Pax," I said, and Nonny agreed, bobbing her head up and down.

"I didn't have enough hands to bring the cake and other food with me. Perhaps the boys would like to go with me down to the palace kitchen and help me?" I wondered.

"I'll go get them." Nonny turned to get the boys.

"It's okay. I know where Jet's room is. Can I?" I touched her arm gently.

She paused and looked up with a small smile and a nod. "Sure."

The girls became absorbed in the presents and the pretty wrapping paper. They kept busy picking each box up, shaking it, and telling the other what they thought was inside.

"Nonny, you don't look well," I told her quietly. She shrugged and put a finger to her lips. I looked at her strangely as she moved before me, so her hands were right in front of her. Then, motioned behind her and mouthed, "Cameras and speakers. Shh."

She opened her eyes big as my expression changed, cautioning me to act normal.

Barely nodding that I understood, I patted her arm and moved around her to find the boys. I sure hoped the bathroom had nothing in it because I would drag Nonny in there later to talk!

I paused at Jet's bedroom door. It was closed. I would've liked to tell Nonny it probably wasn't a good habit to allow children to play behind closed doors. But, of course, it wasn't my place, but as a grandmamma, I could make that suggestion, right?

I barely heard the boys, who were talking to each other quietly. Another thing children rarely do unless they are up to something.

"You can come to stay with us." It was a voice I didn't know, so I assumed it was Pax.

"I want to. I don't like it here." I heard Jet tell him.

"Well, come back with us," Pax reiterated.

"What about all the stuff they make me learn here as a stupid Royal?" Jet said sarcastically. Oh, how I missed the youthfulness of children. Vampires' minds grew much quicker than their bodies. Children needed to be children!

"We also have school stuff of some sort," Pax whispered.

"I'll ask." Jet didn't sound too convinced that he could go.

"If they say no, we can come up with other plans." Pax was confident there was a way.

"Like what?" Jet wondered.

The girls came barreling down the hall to find me. "Grandmamma! There you are. Can we open the presents now?" they yelled as they came down the hall.

The door opened, and Pax stood looking at me. And he didn't look like any five-year-old.

"How long have you been here?" he demanded.

"I just got here and was about to knock." He didn't look very pleased. "I was going to ask Jet and you to go to the palace kitchen to help me bring the cake and food."

"I don't eat food." Pax didn't say that sweetly.

"Then don't help. I assume you're Pax and a friend of Jet's?" I knew that, but introductions were still required. I put my hand out for him to shake it. He looked at it and turned to Jet.

"Do you want to help her?" he asked Jet.

Jet looked at me and wasn't happy about being caught in the middle. He shrugged.

"Jet? I need you. Grandmamma always needs her little man, Jet," I coaxed him.

"He isn't little, and he isn't a man," Pax answered for Jet. No wonder Amy didn't like him! I wondered how, in God's name, Nonny let this kid into her house and around her family.

"I beg to differ," I retorted. "You and I are not off to a good start. How old are you?"

"Thirteen." He held his head high.

"Hmm." That was all I could come up with for him.

"Come on, Jet. You like my cooking. I made your favorite," I told him because I had!

"If he is coming, I'm coming," Pax informed me.

"Great. I'll let you carry the cake." Maybe you'll fall and land in it and get it all over your perfectly mean face. A little sweetness wouldn't hurt!

Being the Oracle had its advantages here. No one could read my mind! Other than the smoke, people, of course. But that was different. That was safe!

* * *

Pax's entire demeanor was different around Nonny. That answered my question of why she let him visit. He was extremely polite when she was around. I couldn't help myself and finally ask after watching a movie, and most of us had popcorn and snacks. "What brings you to play with someone so much younger than you?"

Pax glared at me before Nonny turned to look at him. "Because there are not a lot of children where I'm. Jet is an amazing friend. He teaches me as much as I teach him. He's smart, and we enjoy one another. Isn't that right, Jet?" He looked over, satisfied with his response.

"Yep," Jet said and went to sit by his friend. He had sat on the floor with the rest of us to enjoy the snacks during the show.

"They get along so well." Nonny agreed with the boys.

"Well, I guess it is good to have someone," I said, a bit dryly.

"Like Micah and me?" Amy asked.

“Yes, ma’am,” I told her. “Just like you and Micah.” The girls hugged one another. Now that was what I would expect. They were too cute! Jet and Pax looked at the girls in disgust.

“Having a soft side is not an inferior quality,” I told them.

“Yes. It is. We are strong and tough. We are leaders,” Pax told me.

“Anyone can be a leader,” I argued with him. “The best leaders I have seen are compassionate, respected, and consistent with their people.”

He snorted, “Maybe for humans.” I looked at Nonny to scc if shc was disgusted with his behavior.

“Of course, I mean you no disrespect, Mary.” Rats… he knew!

“Pax does not know what it is like being around humans other than us, of course. His clan, being so out of the loop and old school, I would’ve thought them to be more primitive. It is the opposite. Kind of weird, but a good weird. I was much more frightened of many of the vampires when I first arrived here, as you may recall.” Nonny reminded me.

“I remember. And I also agree that is strange,” I said, looking at Pax. He didn’t flinch.

The girls had tired of our boring conversation. “Is it present time, Grandmamma?” They had planned to speak the question together.

“You bet!” I said with enthusiasm. “Although I didn’t bring one for Jet’s friend, Pax.”

“I don’t need a present,” he said. “Jet makes these visits here all I need.”

“Well, uh, I guess I’ll go get the gifts.” But, again, I didn’t know where to go with that conversation. I sure wished he weren’t here, though!

“We’ll get them!” The girls both jumped up and went to the table where I had left the gifts.

“After presents, we can do cake,” Amy told Micah as they walked back. Nonny and I smiled at each other.

“Precious, aren’t they?” she asked me.

“Barf,” Jet said.

“Oh, Jet!” Nonny laughed. I sighed.

Both the girls set the boxes down on the floor by my feet. "They have our names on them, but I want you to give them to us," Amy directed.

"Okay. How about I give each one of you your gift, and then you can open them together?" They all nodded, and I handed each one their gift.

"Wait," I told them. "There's one thing I need to tell you before you open them." They stopped in their tracks. They all looked at me curiously.

"Grandmamma is going to be going away." My heart filled with sadness.

Nonny sat up. "What? Why?"

"Yes, Grandmamma. Why?" Amy asked sadly.

"Because I have to go help, Mandy, and Buddy. You remember them?" The children all shook their heads.

"They are part of this family. Mandy is your relative, and Buddy is our family dog." I smiled, trying to show that this was a good thing.

"You have a dog?" Jet asked.

"I do. And he is an extraordinary dog. But that doesn't mean I won't be back to visit as often as I can." So I spoke to each one.

Nonny spoke under her breath, and I didn't catch it. "What?" I asked her.

"She said," Pax spoke for her, "you're fortunate, and she wishes she could go, too."

Nonny looked a little green at being not only heard but also outed.

Pax gave her an innocent look. "Oh. Did you not mean to be heard?" I wanted to slap him. He played the victim so well!

"It's okay, Pax. I was thinking about the warm summers and other things," Nonny trailed off.

"But you can still visit?" Amy asked.

"Absolutely!" I told her.

"Can we come to visit you?" Amy wondered.

"Umm. Now that I don't know. With how special you are and you being so young, I'll probably have to make extra visits here." I said it, but I knew that once I was gone, I was completely gone. In my heart, I knew I wouldn't be brought back here. It was a straight-out white lie.

"But that is what is so special about your gifts!" I told them excitedly. Nonny remained quiet and stared at me. I needed to get her into the bathroom for some conversation soon!

"Can we open them?" Jet asked, playing with a corner that he had already partially ripped.

"Open!" I yelled.

They all tore into the gift wrap. Moments later, their enthusiasm diminished as they each held their colorful journals.

"Well, don't be too excited over the present." I wasn't upset. A book of any kind would not be top on the list for any child.

"What is it?" Jet asked in disgust.

"Jet." Nonny looked at him and shook her head at him.

"Extraordinary journals." I hoped my enthusiasm would at least work for Amy.

"Look at the amazing picture on the front. They are incredibly special. Feel them." I encouraged each one. Thankfully, they complied. Not only did they feel the colors that seemed to bulge out of the cover, but they outlined the black lines. I couldn't have asked for more perfection for the finale of the spell. It had been completed. I exhaled a heavy sigh of relief.

"I like it," Amy said.

"It's not bad, I guess," Jet stated.

Micah still didn't get it, but didn't want to hurt my feelings. "It is pretty."

"These are journals you can draw in or write in. They are special! Whatever brings you happiness, write it down! Draw a picture! That way, as you grow older, you can look back on these days and remember the good times and the bad! Write and draw it all."

"What a great idea." Nonny agreed with me. "Like a memory book. I wish I had written more in my life. I would love to look back." She thought for a moment. "Micah, your mom used to do that. She had the most amazing journal, and she shared it with me sometimes. I wonder whatever happened to it?" She closed her eyes, thinking. "Who knows?" She opened her eyes and shrugged.

"My mom had one like this?" Micah asked as the children looked on.

"Yes. It held all her deepest secrets. She wrote in it every day." Nonny spoke now to all the children.

"Interesting. I didn't know that." I told Nonny.

"Yes. Jade went through a lot of journals," Nonny said matter-of-factly.

"What about when I finish the last page of this one? Will I get another one?" Amy quizzed me.

"You'll get as many as you need. As many as any of you need." I motioned to them all. "So, you let Grandmamma know when I need to get you another one."

"Can't they use any kind of book to write in?" Pax half-snorted, obviously bored with the conversation. He couldn't see what the interest was anymore and probably wasn't too enthused that Jet had changed his mind and acted as it seemed kind of cool now.

"I want my Grandmamma's books," Amy told him as she came and crawled into my lap.

"That's the spirit, Amy. I'll make beautiful pictures on the front of each one. We can even number them so that when you're older, you'll know the order."

"Boring. But, whatever," Pax said. "Wanna go play in your room, Jet?"

Jet again looked torn. He was an easily manipulated child, I feared. "Not so fast. We have cake still to do."

"Maybe I'll go for a bit." Pax got up to leave. "All this eating of nasty things is making me think some blood is needed to make me feel better. Too bad you don't have a kitchen in this place." He looked at Nonny.

She shrugged. "Sorry, Pax. Come back soon."

"Oh, I will. You can count on it." He looked at Jet. "See you soon."

"Okay. Bye." Jet didn't get up and walk him out, which pleased me.

"Cake. Cake. Cake," Amy chanted. Micah looked away, uninterested. Vampires!

"Sorry, Micah. I wasn't thinking. I should've grabbed something you would like from the refrigerator downstairs."

"It's okay." She was already way beyond her years.

We sang birthday songs and cut the cake, and then I pulled Nonny after me to the bathroom and shut the door.

"What is going on?" I said, out of pure concern.

"With what?" she asked, knowing very well what I meant.

"Here! With Pax, and Jet, and you! You look terrible, Nonny!" I said in a loud whisper.

"You're the one getting to leave." She put her hand up so I wouldn't talk. "Mary, I know you're concerned, but I'm telling you right now, do not ask or tell me anymore. I'm not protected," she said, motioning to her head. Of course! Someone would read her mind if they were around here. Prodding her memory!

"Come with me, Nonny." I pleaded with her anyway.

She opened the door and left, as her reply.

With another sigh, I looked at myself in the mirror. There was danger here, and I was going to expose it. I had to get out of here to do it, though. I would let Grant know as soon as possible that I needed to leave. Even if I had to tell him, it was for medical reasons. I would get the books Jade wanted and wrap everything up I needed. My bags would be off-limits, and I would take with me what I needed and be gone before anyone knew! All I had left to handle was talking to Jade and wishing my family farewell!

Chapter Eight

Nonny

I had enough, and everyone knew it. My thoughts were no longer my own. My children were taken from me most of the day. They were barely seven years old and given no time to be children.

Amy suffered as well. She wanted me more and more, and Jet wanted me less and less. It was time for something to give.

"Grant." He sat on the couch, studying some books he had brought home. "Grant. Can you put the books down? Just for a moment." I reached out and pulled the book from his hand. He let me.

He stared at me. "Is this about what Kiryana and the others have already told me?"

"It's not fair that I can't keep my thoughts to myself." It made me sad I couldn't have these talks with my husband without him knowing everything already.

He tried to make the usual argument out of it. "You're telling me it isn't fair. You're my wife. This is unfair." His ploy at making the conversation light didn't work as usual.

"Grant, I can't. Amy can't." I looked away because he was still so handsome. I felt so mousy next to him now. Everything about me was hollow. I loved him, but I had lost everything about me.

"Can't what? I want to hear it, Nonny. I know things have been hard for us. It certainly isn't easy being around all these perfect soulmates. We can't help that." He forced the words out.

"We can. We can leave." The words left my mouth for the first time. I had thought about those words for years. The entire clan knew how I felt, but my happiness didn't matter. Only the children mattered. I became hopeful in my plea for a moment.

"We can't, Nonny. I can't," Grant shouted.

"Shh, the children are here… for once." I reminded him.

I couldn't believe I said those words, but I did. "I'm leaving, Grant. And I'm taking the children with me."

He grabbed me by the shoulders. "You can't! They won't let you. I won't let you." He sounded more hurt than angry.

"I'm not a hostage here, Grant. Don't make it that way. I have a family outside of these walls, as do you. Remember that!" I thought of Mary and her freedom. I heard from her rarely, and it sucked being here without her now, even more so.

"I need my family. The children are old enough and have been emotionally tough through all this, as I have, please, Grant. Amy isn't doing well. Can't you see? Our daughter needs a break from here. Jet deserves to know his other grandparents. Maybe we can arrange a visit to your mom, or have her visit us? Please, Grant! I love you, but I need this. We need this!" I cried, and it shocked me when Grant pulled me to him.

"I love you, Nonny." He sounded utterly deflated. "My life is here. My responsibility is here." Then, pulling me back from him, he finally came clean. "I see what you see. It's just…." He ran his hand through his hair as he always did when riled up. "The clan has all these rules, especially for the Royal family."

Feeling hopeful, I tried to compromise. "What if it was just until the children were better? Couldn't you speak on behalf of them?"

"Perhaps… I don't know. What about us? And Jet, he is…." Grant didn't want to judge his son, but I could see the conflict in his eyes. "He may be a handful or something."

"Then we would come back! I won't put him in harm's way or harm's way in front of him. You could come to see us on your breaks. Let our children get to know my parents. Lie to them and then have someone fix their memory again." I could feel the excitement of knowing that there was a slight chance of possibility brewing here. "Our marriage is essential to me. Top priority. But we both know it isn't getting easier or better."

He shook his head. "I don't know what happened," Grant spoke honestly.

"Well, this isn't normal for any of us. We have hope and love and children together. Fight for me, Grant. Fight for all of us. I'll promise and do whatever I have to. Just give us some time away from here. Maybe it will do Jet good. I know it will be good for Amy and me. Remind everyone that these kids have my blood in them also, and that has to be nurtured as well." My blood still ran in them.

Finally, Grant pulled me back to him and kissed me, like he hadn't kissed me in perhaps years. Again, I felt the love, the commitment, and I felt the one that my heart and soul had fallen for, the old Grant.

"Okay, Nonny. Somehow, I'll make them see. You're right. No one is a prisoner here. I'll talk to Tristan and Jade first. After that, the Elders will have their say, but enough time and loyalty have passed that it will be their final decision. The Elders will most likely set the rules, though. Speaking of Jade, when was the last time you two had time together?" Grant wondered.

"Jade is too busy for me. Rarely do we get together, and it is only for Micah and Amy to visit. She's the Queen, and I'm just a mother of some Royal children. Nothing more." It was sad how Jade's and my relationship had become all but nonexistent. I didn't blame her, but I also didn't feel any compassion for her choice not to give her best friend time. How hard was that? Then, with that kind of thinking, I felt ashamed and reminded myself of her duties. I wouldn't want them. "I miss her as I miss you. It was glamorous in the olden days." I confessed.

"Everything about our lives has changed," Grant whispered in my ear as he held me against his chest.

"I know. I never knew things would change so much. And the Drobny…" Did I dare continue?

"What about them?" Grant asked.

"Pax is here a lot, and it seems to get weirder and weirder around here. Jet and he… I don't know."

"You can't go throwing judgment on these kids, Nonny. You know nothing about the Drobny. We have to help and accept each other for all kinds of reasons. They accept us and want to be in our lives. We nurture that and pull them closer and teach them the right ways. Otherwise, you end up back in a Keegan situation." I shuddered as he stated that. HeH loved the Drobny, so I had to change the subject.

"When will you go talk to Tristan and Jade?" Playing with the buttons on his shirt, I looked up from under my eyelashes.

"Woman… don't be looking at me like that," he growled in arousal.

"Or what?" I batted my eyes at him. It felt wonderful to be wanted again. It had been a long time since we had shared ourselves in pleasure.

Scooping me up, he took me to the bedroom and locked the door.

"What about the children?" I teased.

"Better be quiet," he said heatedly.

"Then you'd better perform slowly." And that was that -- game on.

* * *

Amy sat in my room, watching me get ready for the day. "Mommy?"

"Yes, sweet pea?" I sat on my vanity chair, applying what little makeup I had -- a daily task to hide the dark circles under my eyes. I don't know if I made them look better or worse! Putting down the makeup, I turned to face Amy directly.

"I like it being just you and me." Shocked by her acknowledgment of pleasure at her brother being gone for a short time, I didn't know what to say.

"Don't get too used to it. It's just one condition the Elders put in place before letting us go back to Idaho for a break. Once he gets back, we'll all be heading out." The stupid condition had held us here at the palace for a couple of extra weeks. I didn't see the reasoning behind Jet having to visit the Drobny Clan before he could leave. But, as I had told Grant, I would meet with their conditions.

"I'm glad I didn't have to go to the Drobny Clan away from you, Mom." Amy looked pretty serious. And of course, I felt the same! "They scare me. Tristan, the Elders, and even Daddy all try to tell me it's all in my head, and I'm not nice. But Mom…" Amy came over and placed her hand on my arm, "no matter what they say in my spell class to help me think of them differently, it doesn't work, and I'm glad!"

"Whoa! Miss Amy." She had my complete attention! "What do you mean? What are they doing to you? Who is doing this to you?" The questions rolled out all as one. Amy looked confused and stepped back.

"You're scaring me, Mommy. Did I say something wrong?" she whined.

Getting up, I took her hand and led her over to the side of the bed so we could both sit down and talk.

"You have done nothing wrong. Who is there during these 'teaching spells' to help you?" I would've to ask the questions one by one.

"A few Elders, and sometimes that Drobny lady. I especially don't like it when she's there. It's uncomfortable because she stares me down like I have done something wrong! I don't think I have. Do you?" She looked up under her long lashes at me.

"Amy, the day you do something wrong will be a first." I tried to reassure her the best that I could. Finally, she smiled up at me with hope in her eyes.

"Is there anything else you don't like that they're doing to you or your brother that you don't feel okay about?" Amy thought a moment before answering.

"Well, mostly, it is Drobny stuff to me. Jet sometimes goes off with Pax, when he's here, and a couple of other Drobny to the ritual room. He told me about it only once, and that was the first time they did it. He said they do some cool stuff down there that our people don't do."

Did he give you any examples? I wondered.

"Umm… he just said he learned some spell stuff and that they sometimes did spells with him. He said he didn't know what they meant because he was just told to do stuff, and he did. But, you know, with Pax around, Jet does anything Pax tells him to." Amy frowned.

Sighing heavily, I pulled Amy to me. "Well, let's just have our stuff ready to go so when Jet comes back, we can leave. You're going to love your grandparents, and they are going to adore you." I felt partly responsible now for letting Pax become like a member of my household. I didn't know what anyone's intentions were, but I became relentless to get myself and my children out of there!

Amy pulled away. "I'm nervous about going away from here. We have never been away from here! What if we do something bad?"

"Amy, that is the least of my worries. I think getting you two away from here for a while is a good thing, especially to meet your other grandparents. Also, I think the fact that you're thinking about how to act shows you're ready to be responsible outside of here."

Amy processed what I told her. "Even Jet?"

"Even Jet," I lied. I would keep a much tighter leash on that kid! Another condition would be that a Shadow Night guard wouldn't be far. So, in Jet's case, that was good. In my case not so good. I would probably never feel what freedom was like again.

"We have to keep to the story they have pounded in our heads the last several years, that your dad is in the military, and we have been stationed far away. He is a special secret military man, and because of that, where we were is kept top secret." I reiterated the story that Amy must have heard a million times.

"I know." She rolled her eyes but smiled, anyway.

"Do you think Grandmamma could come to Idaho to see us, too? I need another pretty journal." She looked away in thought. "And I think Jet is getting close. He left his book here. Pax wouldn't let him take it. Would it be bad to sneak and look?" Amy rubbed her hands together mischievously.

"How would you like Jet to look through your journal?"

Amy's eyes opened wide. "No!" she said.

"So, there's your answer." I might peek, but I didn't want Amy looking. God only knows what Jet put in his. I gave them both kudos, though, especially Jet. I never thought he would take to writing and drawing in it so diligently. It surprised the heck out of me!

"I'll have to help you pack as well. You can bring whatever toys and items you can't live without, but we probably won't bring a lot of your clothes along. Just enough to get us to Idaho clean. I can introduce you to the world of shopping!" Now that sounded exciting! I had missed shopping a lot! "We can all use some new clothes."

"Shopping… like what I see on TV?" Amy asked.

"Oh, my goodness, yes! And there are parks and toys, and so much to show you! I can't wait! You and Jet are going to love it!" I couldn't contain my energy and pulled Amy up and whirled her around.

"Wee!" Amy screeched.

"What is all the excitement about?" Grant stood in the doorway, looking pleased with what he saw.

"Hi, Daddy!" Amy wiggled out of my arms to jump into her daddy's.

"What has gotten into my goofy girls?" He gave Amy an angel kiss.

"Mom said we are going shopping!" she explained, still excited.

Grant tilted his head back and laughed out loud. "Oh, my. Say no more, little one. I completely understand now."

"Have you been shopping before, Daddy?" Amy wondered.

Grant peered over Amy's head. "Once or twice." He winked at me.

"I was coming to let you know that Jet should be back in about three days. So." He scrunched his face up, looking sad. "If you're still set on going, which I see you are."

Amy wrapped her arms around his neck and pulled him in for a hug. "Can't you come with us?"

"Daddy has to work, like always. But I'll come and visit you often, Princess. When Daddy is gone a lot from here at the palace, I'm actually among all the humans you'll be around."

"So, maybe this is a wonderful vacation, Daddy. We'll get to see you even more?" This little one was spot on!

"Perhaps," Grant told her and kissed her cheek as he set her back down.

Amy darted from the room. "I'm going to go pack!" she yelled out behind her.

Grant came over and pulled me into his arms. Things had almost gone back to being normal since the talk of us leaving. The heavy feeling and arguments had all but disappeared.

"You smell like Heaven," he muttered as he pulled my hair away from my neck and kissed my neck tenderly. I could feel the heat rising in me, and my stomach flipped around like a schoolgirl with butterflies. Then he nipped my neck with his teeth, I think. I suppose it could've been his fangs. Sometimes, the fangs came out when he became excited, no matter how hard he tried to hold them in. It was scary at first, but now I found it erotic. A romance novel that comes to life; hell yes, I played on it!

He pulled me backward with him toward the open door. Gently shutting and locking it, he nipped my neck. His hands were at my breasts. Then, with a rip, my shirt and bra were lying on the floor. I wasn't sure how long my knees would hold me in this erotic state of mind, so I placed my hands on his shoulders for support.

He nipped and kissed me from my neck down, across my breast, down my stomach, not missing an inch anywhere.

"Oh God, Grant. I'm going to fall over," I whispered.

He ran his tongue across my belly, right above my panty line.

My hips moved toward him, out of control. My mind told me I wanted more, as my fingers dug into his shoulders.

The snap to my jeans released and I felt them being pulled down as he continued with his nips and kisses along the way. Finally, I stepped out of my jeans and undies, fully exposed.

"You're so beautiful, Nonny," he murmured to me, and then I felt his tongue trace up my thigh and stop at the heat of my desire.

It was a night I would remember and take with me to the grave!

* * *

Grant asked me for the hundredth time, "You're sure you have everything you need?" shortly before he had to leave us with my parents in Idaho.

"Yes," I reassured him. I had contacted my parents the same day he told me. Jet would return to the palace to come to Idaho. He had stayed with the Drobny longer than I had expected. My folks were beyond excited and remodeled three bedrooms at their house so that we could live there for now. I wasn't sure whether we would stay there the whole time. It all depended on how Jet and Amy acted and grew. I was just glad to be home with them.

Putting them into the school system hadn't appealed to anyone at the Shadow Night, so I had to put the kids in an online school course as one of their conditions. They both understood that it would be material they would've learned years ago, as they had already excelled up to high school standards.

Grant stared at me, not knowing what else to say.

I pulled him into me. "I've got this, Grant. I feel so much better already, being here. Even the children are enjoying it here." He squeezed me tightly.

"I know, and that helps." He kissed my head. "But all of you don't have the safety of the palace."

There was another direction I could go with that comment, but II didn't comment to keep the peace and not argue during our goodbye. "We are safe. There are plenty of guards around. And remember, we may even see you more." I wanted to leave everything on a positive note.

"True." Last night we had gone over how much more we would have that possibility, with me being in the continental States with him now. Of course, he would be overseas as well, but he'd be in the States a lot of time, too.

Pulling away, I looked around for the children so they could say goodbye as well. They were waiting next to my parents in front of Grant's Hummer. The day before, we had gone and purchased a car for me. Jet had wanted a shiny red truck, and Amy wanted a newer yellow Volkswagen bug with a flower on the hood. "But Mom, it's so cute," she had pleaded.

Grant opted for comfort and endurance and bought a beautiful, blue-colored Land Cruiser. I was happy, and after a luxurious ride home in it, both children had turned their frowns upside down!

"Come, give Daddy some love before he leaves." I motioned for the kids to come over, and my parents followed as well. Grant hugged and kissed the children and shook my father's outstretched hand.

"We'll take care of your family," he told Grant. It was the oddest thing I heard since our homecoming over a week ago. My dad had been my hero, and I was his little princess. It was like we had all matured overnight and had become close on a much different level. Before Grant, my family had always been just my mom and dad. And here I had my family now.

I hadn't realized I had been staring at my parents, and a giant sigh left my chest. "What's that about?" Grant asked, looking at me peculiarly.

"Memories. Life is all about memories, old and new." I smiled up at him and rose onto my tiptoes. He met me halfway and kissed me hard. "I love you so much," he whispered in my ear. My heart was light, even though he was leaving. For the first time in so long, life felt great!

Chapter Nine

Mary

For the past four years, I had watched my grandchildren grow up through their journal writings and pictures. I was at peace, knowing they were okay and away from the palace. But Grant had been by frequently, not once letting me know Nonny had taken the children to live with her parents in Idaho. That part made little sense. He had trusted and sought me out in his time of need twelve years ago. How could he see me as a threat of any kind now? It had to be the Drobny Clan; it had to.

Mandy sat next to me on the couch in my office. "Anything?" She sounded hopeful.

Shrugging and tossing the notes and book on the table, I leaned into the corner of the couch. "I don't know." I was tired, exhausted, and my Oracle's powers had dimmed once I left the palace. I had expected them to grow, but the only thing growing was the gray in my hair and the wrinkles on my face.

Jet had feelings for Micah. It could very well be a soulmate link, but it was hard to be sure with Jet's genetic makeup. I had never asked Grant about his and Nonny's relationship in those terms. He was sure the soulmate bond was coming from the vampire within him, but he was also half-human. Maybe he had just never felt love at first sight. Jet was genuinely taken with Micah, but he kept all those feelings hidden from everyone. Especially from the Drobny, particularly Pax.

Had it not been for Jet now, taking his journal with him on ''summer vacations'' to see his friend Pax, I wouldn't have known much more than that. Jet had figured out that Amy read his journal whenever he wasn't around, so he didn't leave without it anymore. Amy would describe Jet's slow change process, each time he had been away with the Drobny Clan, as dark. He plotted something; she was sure of it. It made me work harder and longer hours at home to figure out how to stop whatever was being brewed.

Amy had become quite distant from her brother, preferring to stay near her mom. The children were forced to keep much of their lives a secret, and a bond was missing between them and their maternal grandparents. However, Amy's descriptions were so keen. It was as if I were there with her.

Mandy set something small and light in my lap. "Where did you find this?" I asked, picking it up in surprise. Buddy looked up from his comfortable spot near the fireplace and came over.

"Woof!" He sniffed the necklace.

"What is it?" Mandy asked. "Is it yours?"

"No… it's… it was Jade's." Deep in thought, I wondered how, after the years, it had been found again and here!

"When Buddy was down yesterday, keeping me company at my house, he pulled it out from somewhere. I forgot to bring it with me last night. It isn't mine, so I thought maybe it was yours."

I held the necklace up and looked at the beautiful detail of the charm. "It was once mine. A long, long time ago. I energized and infused it with Oracle's light to help protect Jade when she was much younger." I smiled, thinking about the time I had spent making it and then the joy of giving it to Jade at the kiosk in the Boise mall.

"Oh?" Mandy was intrigued.

"Buddy, go on," she told the aging dog. He wouldn't leave and looked from me to the necklace several times, like he wanted to tell me something.

"You think you want it?" I asked him. "It's not your style, I would think, Buddy. But I owe you for finding it. I don't think Jade had worn it for some time. At least I don't recall it on her here."

"I would've remembered." Mandy insisted as well.

Buddy whined. "I wish you could tell me what it is you want to say."

"Is there a spell for that?" Mandy asked, completely serious.

I laughed. "No, I can't be a fairy godmother and make animals talk."

She laughed as well. "I wouldn't be surprised if you could."

"Besides, you know that leaving the palace has done something to my Oracle life." I looked down at Buddy. "You and I are getting old."

Mandy's voice became a bit broken up. "Why now?"

"Why now, what?" I knew, but asked anyway.

"All you have ever done is good. You have been the vampires' pawn whenever they needed you. You raised me. I thought you would outlive me, just like in all your other lives," she whispered.

Mandy had given her life up for me. I was different, and she had protected me, as our family had done before. Only she didn't have a husband or children. No legacy. She'd given it all up for me.

"Don't get sappy on me just yet. I'm barely in my prime." Wasn't I?

"Time seems to go faster now, though, for you." She stood up and went over to add another log onto the fire.

"All things have to end. I'm tired of being pulled back and forth and set-in time anew." Wasn't I?

"You have Grant and Nonny and their children. As well as Jade and Tristan and Micah." I set the necklace on the table and went over to Mandy, where she stood with her back to me, silently shaking.

"You have been the daughter I could never keep. You're my life, Mandy." Placing my hand on her back, I wanted to comfort her. But everything about our situation was new, and I didn't know what to tell her or how to handle it myself.

"You're both right." A male voice that sounded somehow familiar startled us both. Mandy and I both jumped in surprise and turned around, preparing for some kind of attack.

"Kade?" My eyes had to be deceiving me. But there he stood. Tall, dark, and handsome, just like any other vampire. Jade resembled him a lot. He was a little taller, and of course, larger. Perhaps even larger than Grant. His features were delicate in a way. The Royals all stood out, ever so slightly.

"Mary. Mandy." He took a bow. "It is indeed I."

"I don't think we've met," Mandy said, out of breath.

"Mandy, this is Jade's older brother, Kade. He, you…" I didn't know who to talk to first.

"It's okay… I died that night. Killed by that demonic asshole Keegan. But not before saving Jade."

"How are you here?" Confusion engulfed me.

"Down there." He pointed to the necklace wrapped around his leg. It was loose, and he seemed fearful of moving and losing it.

Like a light switch going on in both Mandy's and my mind, we both yelled out, "You're Buddy!" He smiled and nodded.

"How come you didn't do that yesterday? Why didn't you do that yesterday?" Mandy asked.

"I can only change, Mary, with this. It is her power that guides it." He made the whole thing sound matter of fact.

"Why did you wait so long?" Then, seeing that he couldn't move, I went over to him and welcomed Kade with a hug.

"Mary?" he asked after I stood back. "Can you move the necklace to a better spot so I can move?"

"Oh! Yes! Of course, will it hurt you?" I couldn't imagine how the whole thing would take place.

"Perhaps. I don't know. I haven't gone back into the dog yet." He cringed.

"I'll be quick, regardless," I promised.

"On the count of three, one… two… three." I whipped it off his leg and up around his neck in seconds.

"That was close," Kade said. "Any longer, and I would've been on the floor."

"So, you controlled yourself?" I wondered.

"I don't know. I fought against it, knowing it wouldn't be long," Kade quipped.

"Mary…" Mandy sounded concerned.

Spinning around to face Mandy, I answered, "Yes?"

"Your hair, it's like it whitened right before my eyes." Her face looked like she had seen a ghost.

"It's because of me," Kade quietly stated behind me.

My hand moved to my throat. I needed to see for myself. I had a large mirror in the office, and I'mble over to it. There, I turned my head to the side. The new white showed like fresh winter snow. I tried to make light of knowing I was now my worst enemy when it came to my destiny. "Job hazard, I guess." Turning around, I smiled meekly at them.

"Perhaps I should go back to being the dog," Kade said with sadness.

"No!" Mandy jumped at him with her arms out. She smoothed her shirt down and tried to correct her outburst. "I mean, you shouldn't change any more than you have to. Stay like this?" Was Mandy blushing?

Kade wasn't dumb, and he picked up on her crush right away. "I wish I could. The longer I hold the magic, the more it's going to age Mary." He smiled, but the sadness was there. Of course, he wished to be in vampire form rather than Buddy, the dog.

"But Mary is aging… what if something happens?" Mandy struggled to find a reason.

"There's a reason I'm here, Mandy. It took time for everything to work out in my favor so I could be here now." He tried to explain it to Mandy as she folded her arms across her chest, closing herself off to any more objections.

I took over. "So, what is the reason, Kade?"

"I'm here to help, of course, without bringing you to your death first." He looked cross, but he wanted to make sure we knew where his allegiance lay. The Shadow Night was, and would always be, his home and where his loyalty forever would remain.

"Have you been in Buddy all this time?" Mandy still wanted to talk about other things in her state of shock. I had moved on; it was of no more concern than what I did or didn't get done yesterday.

"Mandy, perhaps another time we can ask the lesser questions?" I didn't want to sound rude after we'd just had a real heart-to-heart talk, but evidently, my time here on Earth seemed to be limited.

"Yes, of course! I'm so sorry." Mandy looked apologetic.

"It's fine. We are fine, for now. Just food for thought, for later conversation," I told her as I patted her arm. No matter how big or small the gesture, contact with loved ones was a true gift that people didn't realize often enough.

"I think, Mandy, I have a real quick answer to your question." He looked at me to ensure he had my blessing to answer this one question, and I nodded permission. "I mean, I feel like I was born a dog, and then when I saw Grant for the first time, it was like a firework went off in my head, and I became me, trapped in Buddy's body. I had some issues accepting this at first, and all these years have been hard, but the smoke people have worked hard with me to help me overcome the tough times. Then, after a while, things became easier." He nodded, probably thinking back on the last years. "And you all have been so great! And I got to see home again, ever so briefly, and then spend a lot of time with you, Mandy, and then with Mary, when you came back." He smiled at me. "I truly feel blessed, now. I do. I'm working for a greater power."

"Amen to that," I said. "And the smoke people… I don't know how they didn't make you go nuts with their rhyming and whatnot." I shook my head. "They are a mysterious bunch. I can't ever get what I need from them without more questions, and then poof, I'll be back in the real world."

"Yeah, well…" He scratched the side of his face, "you and I are working together, but on different levels." He grinned.

"Not fair!" I said, "But does that mean you can tell me what you know?" Raising my eyebrows toward him. The answer had to be yes!

"Umm, no." He shrugged. "They've told you the universe is unbalanced. If it could be balanced out already with words and certain actions, don't you think that would already have happened?"

"I don't know. I guess." That wasn't what I wanted to hear. "Why does all this have to be so complicated? It should've ended when Tristan bit Jade and took her back to her rightful self and position."

"Okay! Now go with that thought, Mary." Kade seemed to be excited about what I'd said. That threw me. "Ask yourself why. Why isn't everything okay and normal?"

I needed a chair. Sitting back on the couch, I put my head into my hands and closed my eyes. My mind went blank rather than filling with answers. Why? What was I missing?

"Jet and Amy?" I questioned.

"They would've been fine if…." He left me to think again.

Mandy came and sat with me again. "Micah?" she asked Kade.

"Micah is well." He thought about it momentarily before he answered, though.

"Why did you pause then?" I frowned at him.

"Because Jade has a mystery in hand that is tied to the source."

Ahh, the dark side. Who is Micah, and where did she come from? Jade and I had a quick chat before I left, and she'd shared with me some very toxic nightmares. I'd tried to make her feel that's all they were.

"Is Micah at risk?" I asked.

"Not at present." Kade didn't expand.

"The Drobny, I know, is an evil clan. I think they are destroying Jet somehow." I lifted my head for an answer.

"It's not what you think. Honestly, I don't know everything. Just the minimum to go on." He wanted to make that clear to me.

“Okay. But the Drobny are a part of this, and I wasn’t able to protect Jet correctly. So, he is the weak link.” Kade agreed with my thought process. “And Micah is safe for now.” He still nodded. A face flashed in my mind, and it wasn’t from my thoughts. “No!” I covered my face.

“What? Mary? What did you see?” Mandy put her arms around my shoulders.

Kade came over and kneeled in front of me. “What?”

“Jet… drew himself a picture. I… can’t….” I could feel my body shaking.

“What did you see, Mary?” Mandy asked, and I assumed Kade knew what I meant, as he had been around us many times when I had talked to Mandy about what I saw from either Amy or Jet.

Whispering, because I didn’t want to tell them what I saw, “Jet… he drew a picture of himself standing in front of two horrid, hateful beings.” I looked up and stared into Kade’s eyes. “He was smiling and seemed to get congratulated by Keegan and Diamonté.”

Kade didn’t miss a beat. “And there you have it.”

“Jet only recently realized that Amy had been reading his journal during his time away with the Drobny Clan. It wasn’t until this last month or so that I got to see exactly how bad these guys are.” They had wormed their way in, and the Shadow Night Clan had let them. “I’m surprised something damning hasn’t happened already.”

“You aren’t at the Shadow Night palace anymore. So, how can you even be sure something hasn’t happened?” Mandy wondered.

“You’re right.” Then, sitting down heavily into my desk chair, I moaned, “I can’t.”

Kade spoke up. “You’re both wrong. Why do you think everything is falling into place now?”

“So, like tomorrow or the next day, or what are you thinking?” I looked up at Kade with hopes of an end to this.

“That I don’t know for sure. But the children are young and still learning. So, Mary, keep on digging and doing what you’re doing. I’m sure we have seen nothing yet.”

I yawned, suddenly growing exhausted. "Why is evil so hard to kill?"

He shook his head and shrugged. "It's time for me to go." Kade saw my yawn and knew it was because of him.

"I'm sorry." I felt bad. "I don't know how I can be so tired, knowing these hell-raisers are still alive and their blood-sucking spinoffs are all around my family."

"Don't be sorry. Just keep doing what you're doing, and let me help as much as I can. My communications will be limited. So say nothing to Grant or anyone else who comes here."

"What about the twins? Do you protect them still?" He could tell me! All these years, I wondered.

Kade smiled. "You're doing an excellent job, Grandmamma." He undid the necklace, and seconds later, he became Buddy once again. He looked at me through eyes I now recognized, and I swore he smiled.

I could live with that for now.

* * *

I can't believe the mess Jet caused during our sixteenth birthday party today. He ruined everything for me! I hate him so much! I wished he had never come back from the Drobny this last time! He had spent time at the palace as well, and even Micah made me feel some sense of betrayal toward her. She had made the trip with Jet and Pax back to Idaho with Dad, Aunt Jade, and Uncle Tristan. It was supposed to have been a grand party. Now, they're all gone, except for my mom and me. We've left my grandparents' house and have been forced into some morgue for the night. Clean-up patrol was busy with making sure we had never existed a day here.

It was the biggest mistake of Jet's life, yet he came out the hero. Tricks. They all played his tricks. Now they all thought I was as loony as they played me. I guess a better word would be victims. And where did all the Drobny come from? I can't even explain that. The events turned into some blood orgy at the house. Thankfully, it was all umbilical cord blood and not from human sacrifices; the horror on my grandparents' faces. The experience was surreal. Whatever was in that stuff, I wanted it. A part of me wanted it bad. I hated that part of me, and I didn't understand why, so I drank when I had to. I loved human life and the surrounding feelings. I felt much safer here than I ever had at the palace. I didn't know a life without Drobny, and I had only known the stories that the Shadow Night Clan had told me of times before Keegan killed so many of the clansmen and almost every one of the Royal Family. As the Drobny came closer to the inner circle, the less the stories were told. Almost like they were taboo.

It has been a long time since I've seen Grandmamma. She won't be at the palace anymore, either. I have nothing to go back there to. It isn't fair! Let them go be there and let me and my mom go to Grandmamma. She would keep us safe. I'm sure of it. I don't want to be around Jet. I see a shadow around him now, and the way Micah was into him made me sick. I got called out for being jealous of them. Jet said I was jealous that Micah was his. Now, tell me that doesn't sound odd!

Anyway, the party was a disaster in my book. Dad was glad about seeing Jet turn into an adult vamp. I may be a late bloomer. But, again, what I saw was nothing like that and nothing to celebrate. Tristan and Jade didn't seem to mind what was going on. Jade and my mom mostly talked about us kids the whole time, until the Drobny showed up, saying they had unique gifts for the birthday kids, us! Jet told them it was about time they showed up, and I wasn't sure if any of the Royals had known they were coming, but they looked happy to see the Drobny, taking drink after drink from the cups they were serving. Finally, Pax thrust one at me, and I took it, smiling warily, and pretended to drink from it. From what I can remember, there was no gift for either of us regarding material things.

My mom had been freaked out, as were her parents. Easily taken and harshly tied up so they wouldn't be a problem. I followed my mom and ran out of the house, thankfully having my hippy bag slung over my shoulder, as I always did. I would be lost without my journal and a few other mementos that I loved. We didn't get far as Drobny Clan members grabbed us and took us to this morgue, telling me in particular that I needed to let it out. What the hell?

I'm so over this, and I want my life back. I'm sitting here with my mom in this nasty morgue. I don't even have her to talk to. I don't know what they gave her, but she is sleeping soundly. They told me that if I didn't sit here quietly and behave, they would take matters into their own hands. And you know what, it was the first time I saw the shadows brewing around all of them, not just Jet. Why I could see and feel something that my clansmen could not, I didn't know.

* * *

That's because you're protected, my sweet Amethyst, I thought to myself. Amy's journal writing had awakened me. Sadness filled my heart. The time drew near, my body deteriorating, and Amy's journal entry confirmed it.

Buddy, or Kade, it was still hard for me to pick one or the other, looked at me from the side of my bed.

"I think Jet has been released." I questioned him, rather than letting Kade know. He threw his head up and barked, then whined.

"They are heading back to the palace. Jet's not protected, is he? I need to end this once and for all." Throwing the covers back, I got out of bed and headed for the office. I had work to do.

Chapter Ten

Jade

I looked from Tristan to the necklace Marissa gave me when I was young and human, in disbelief that this treasure still existed. "I wondered what had happened to this. Where did you find it?"

"Grant has had it a little while," Tristan said with little emotion.

"Huh? Why? He knew it was mine." That didn't sound like something Grant would do. "He kept it on purpose?"

Tristan nodded. "He said he found it at Mary's house last time he was there. He had forgotten about it. When I was in his quarters, he was going through some stuff; it had fallen on the floor." Tristan sat on the massive black sectional in our quarters. It was quite comfortable. "Too much going on." He kicked his shoes off to relax. "Come over here and relax with me a bit."

I saw the look of desire in his eyes. We haven't had any alone time in forever! Plopping down next to him, I still held the necklace in my hand. Tristan wrapped me in his arms and started kissing my neck.

"Does Mary know Grant took it?" Then, pulling my arm out from my cocoon, I dangled the necklace in front of us.

"I don't know. I didn't give the necklace much thought." He sounded irritated. "I knew it was yours, and I thought I would give it back to you. It's not like you need it."

"No. It's funny how things show up." He grabbed my wrist and pulled my hand back down to his legs.

"I need something," he growled at me and sucked and nibbled on my ear. I wanted to talk, but he wanted no part of it.

"You're such an animal." Complying and snuggling closer to him, I dropped the necklace on the floor.

"And you're just figuring that out?" He teased.

I bit his neck in various areas, and before I knew it, he'd flipped me onto my back beneath him. The look in his eyes seemed like he wanted to eat me whole.

"You look a little hungry." Teasing back, I tried hard to wiggle out of his grasp.

"What's wrong?" Tristan was strong, and I couldn't budge.

"There's a buffoon on me." I played.

"A buffoon?" He bent down to murmur in my ear. "Name-calling is going to get you in trouble."

"I'm counting on it." I was busy replying and licking his neck.

"Damn, Jade. You're driving me insane already," Tristan groaned as he ground his hips into mine.

"Tristan?" I knew this wasn't the time to try holding another discussion. But the thought often popped into my head that it would be nice to have more children. I think he responded with some kind of animal growl.

"How come so few vampires have been blessed with tyros here at Shadow Night?" Of course, I meant us primarily.

"I don't know." He stopped and looked at me with mischief in his eyes. "Maybe we are being blessed now, so let's not chance missing it and talk later."

"Point taken." Grabbing his glutes in my hands, I gave a firm squeeze and pulled him against me. Better not to leave anything to chance.

* * *

It was ritual morning, with the Royals and Elders only. But somehow, Pierce from the Drobny Clan had been allowed into this mix several years prior. Now, he was petitioning for several more Drobny clansmen to be welcomed in, "For the benefit of strength."

Tristan and I utterly opposed the idea. This had never been the way with my parents or any of the Royal line. Tristan and I kept presenting our arguments to the Elders only when the Drobny wasn't present, but I'm sure Pierce knew our feelings. In even further detail, Tristan told me that the ways of the Shadow Night were definitely in a state of change during our private times. It was as if they were in charge, and not us. While we remained on the pedestal, I felt, as did Tristan, that the Elders had taken over, and we hadn't known how to stop them. I minded, but I didn't except, with matters like this revolving around the Drobny, I cared.

"My family has always been the only one in this room. The only exception being a new soulmate or new Elder." I didn't want to appear arrogant to Pierce as his eyes drilled into me at that moment. But I had to make a stand here. I didn't argue with them, other than they had been given access to my family's rights. I was close to several, and we all were family, but this?? When would enough be enough?

"This room is still filled with a select group, Jade. Your Royal entities are what we all hold on to foremost. Yet, as you know, a time of change and rebirth has come upon us. We were once a single group, and now there's at least one other. Who knows if there are more." The Elder spoke gently but with purpose.

"I know. Trust me, I know of the change." My tone, quite dry, said it all. "I wonder why there have to be select clans and not just the one. Why must we separate if we are of one race? Why have they not opted to unite with us and defend the Shadow Night as one? Why have you not demanded that? My being Royal means nothing more than merely a lifeline." Tristan placed his hand on my arm. I hoped it was moral support and not a request to be quiet. I wasn't done, though.

"Jade." Pierce stood up. "Your Royal Highnesses, Elders." He bowed to us all. "If I may?" He asked the Elders' permission to address me. Several nodded, giving him the go-ahead to continue.

"First, your Highness, Jade, the Drobny Clan is that. It is another clan. We are learning the Shadow Night ways now, but we have been a secret society, distinguished by a lifestyle with no leadership and direction. We have no history that we know of ever being handed down. We know nothing other than what we have told you. It is our goal to intertwine with all of you and be one society." Pierce paused, wanting what he'd said to sink in.

"I don't think this is the time or place to throw crazy talk and theories into the discussion, as you have done, Pierce. While we are brothers of a race, if there's something on your mind, it needs to be addressed properly, just like anything else." Heatedly, I chose my words as carefully as I could. "You ask for more Drobny clansmen to be present where my family once sat. That is up for discussion here. I'm telling you no."

"Because you fear change?" he demanded.

"How dare you question the way our existence has been when you do not even know your history," I shouted at him.

Tristan pulled me back as I had stood, overthrowing my chair. "Without Jade, none of us would still be here."

"And you're the one to talk?" he said snidely.

"That's enough, Pierce." Tristan kept his voice calm. "Don't forget who you're talking to. She is our Queen."

"Amen." Several Elders responded. That surprised me.

"Forgive me." Pierce sat back down. He looked like a kid who had been caught stealing candy from the candy jar. I looked at Tristan. Something else was going on here. I could feel it.

"This room isn't right," I stated, instantly regretting the statement.

"Perhaps it's you, Jade," an Elder said. I didn't know who, but I looked around for the speaker.

"Excuse me?" This entire conversation was way out of hand.

"I'll heed the Queen's request that more Drobny cannot take part where I do, for now. My apologies for making you upset." Pierce had collected himself and once again looked completely prim and proper. I couldn't keep up with the random thoughts and feelings I experienced. Other than it felt like I had been on trial just then.

I don't know how long I stood there looking like a fool with my mouth open. Finally, Tristan pulled me back down into my chair.

"Are we ready to discuss the children now?" Elder Brawn said.

"We are," Kiryana spoke up. Had it been her speaking earlier? I felt at such odds with myself.

"Micah?" Elder Brawn spoke.

"Yes," Micah spoke up. She sat at the end of the table with Jet and Amethyst. For a while, I sat and watched the children. I wasn't paying any attention to what questions were being asked and answered by them or the Elders. Often, they would get up and go to a ritual book or Elder and do what was asked. Instead, I watched their body language as if I viewed a movie.

I saw it. I know I did. I wondered who else knew. I wasn't sure if I should be happy or sad or what? Jet was like Grant. Half and half. So what did it mean? Micah looked at Jet from the corner of her eye. She had long eyelashes to help hide her gaze. But a mother knows.

How long had this been going on, and I had missed it? Peeling my eyes away from the kids, I looked at the group. Everyone seemed to be engrossed except Pierce, and he stared at me. Tristan didn't even notice. He looked down at the kids and back at me. Did he know? His eyes told me he did, but what did it matter if he knew?

"Adjourned." Chairs scooted back. I barely heard Elder Brawn end the ritual meeting.

"Tristan, grab Micah and bring her up to our quarters." Hurrying out and up the stairs, I didn't wait for his reply. Instead, I heard Tristan call after me a few times before I was out of his range.

I stopped at the top of the stairs, looked over the balcony, and heard Tristan and Micah before seeing them. They rounded the corner, and I was surprised to see Jet and Amethyst with them as well.

"Shoot!" Ducking down, I went into our room and waited.

The laughter got louder and louder as they climbed the stairs. "Should we wait out here?" Amethyst asked Tristan.

"No. I think it's fine." His voice sounded unsure.

"Damn," I whispered under my breath. I couldn't tell Tristan that I didn't want the rest in here.

They all entered together. Micah ran over and hugged me, as she always did. I bear-hugged her back before she stepped back to stand next to Amethyst and Jet.

"They had plans, and I didn't think this would take long, so they are all here. I hope that is okay?" Tristan asked.

"What have you all got planned?" I directed my question to all three.

"Fighting sessions," Jet blurted out.

"It's not fighting." Amethyst corrected him.

"I get what you mean, protection rounds. I have had a few myself," I admitted. "But I'm just a little rusty now."

"Yeah. And Pax and a few other Drobny are here to have a go before I leave again with them."

"Oh… hmm. Well, that's news to me." I glanced at Tristan and received a nice blow-off look.

"They may even let me go this time." Micah acknowledged with excitement.

I sent another look to Tristan, showing my dismay at being left out of this complete loop of conversation.

"Well, we don't know that right now, sweetheart." Tristan came over and stood next to our daughter, wrapping an arm around her. "That idea was only discussed as we came up the stairs.

Amy looked distant and disgusted; although engaged in their conversation. They were supposed to be best friends, after all. By her expression, she looked more like the odd one out now.

“What about you, Amy?” I asked her, bringing her full attention from her thoughts.

“Yeah, no. Not me. The only place I venture is in the States, where my grandparents are, and where I can get a little reality from this place of confinement.

“And when will that be?” I had often wondered that myself.

Tristan frowned and shook his head at me to leave that conversation alone. Again, being the Queen of some place sure made me feel as if I remained in the dark. I frowned back at him.

He mouthed “later” to me, and I rolled my eyes.

“If you all don’t mind, before I let you go, I would like a moment of Micah’s time alone?” It hadn’t come out as a request.

“Even me?” Tristan asked in a rather hurt voice.

“Yes, dear. Just for a moment.” I smiled meekly at him. Finally, he got the point and escorted Jet and Amethyst out.

“She won’t be long. I want a quick mother-daughter talk.” I got the brush-off from them as they exited the door.

“Shut it, please,” I hollered after them. Someone did.

Micah sat on the sofa, now looking perplexed.

“What?” She didn’t sound happy. “Couldn’t this have waited? I have plans. And I also don’t know when the Drobny are leaving so I can go back with Jet.

“Yes, about that. It isn’t exactly what I called you up here for, but I guess it plays into it.” It was the truth in some parts.

“Well then, let’s get it done so I can be on my way. As you already know, they’re waiting for me.” Micah sounded cross.

“Well, first, I’m putting my foot down about you going to the Drobny.” Then, pausing, I waited for the outburst soon to follow.

“It’s already planned, and even Kiryana and some of the other Elders think it’s a great idea!” Micah became outraged.

"Well, guess what? I'm Mom, and I say no. You have no business going with a boy and that clan. There's something not right."

"Something not right, according to who? You? Miss Highness Majesty?" She may as well have slapped me in the face.

"What is going on with you and Jet?"

Micah hunkered down on the couch. Like a light switch flipping, she had gone from tiger to lamb. "I don't know what you're talking about." She crossed her arms in front of her.

"Yeah, well. I was young once too."

"Jet is nothing like Dad. He isn't even a full breed. It isn't like that." She defended her position.

"Well, daughter, tell me exactly how it is." Then, crossing my arms over my chest, I looked at her sternly.

"There's no exactly how it is, Mother." Micah piped back up; the tiger was back.

"Oh, sure there is, Micah."

"Well, I don't know what you want me to say. I'm practically an adult, so…" Her changed demeanor wasn't like her. She was so obvious to read, but I held back. I wanted her to talk to me, not clam up.

"I'm going to visit the Drobny Clan. I have plenty of people to hang out with, and you want to broaden them, and us, you say. Yet, you keep me confined."

"I keep you safe." Micah pushed my buttons. She learned the fine art of manipulation; however, practiced it on the wrong person.

I held up my palm to her because I didn't want to hear any more bullshit. "We don't talk this way to each other, Micah. Stop. Think before you speak. Let me repeat myself to you. I wasn't born yesterday. I was young once too, you know." *I was young more than once,* I thought.

"I know… I know, but you're drowning me. I say I want to go, and you say no. To everywhere." Micah pouted.

"I have to, Micah. That's what you don't want to understand. You're the first Shadow Night Royal to be born."

"No, I'm not! Jet and Amy are," Micah argued.

"You're the first full Royal vampire of the Shadow Night to be born, Micah. Absolutely yes. Yes. There are two others of new Royal blood, but they are different. You know that, and they know, and everyone else knows. The risk of the Shadow Night becoming extinct has lessened because of them, but do not deny your Royal place and what it means." My harsh intentional voice made it crystal clear where I stood on her position as my and Tristan's daughter.

Micah didn't respond and stared at me blankly. Like a deer staring into the headlights of a car, not caring about the outcome of its death.

"Hello?" This talk quickly went from bad to worse.

"I have to go. I don't want them to leave without me." Micah abruptly stood up.

"I didn't realize this conversation was over."

"I'm going where Jet, and even you, have gone and returned safely. I'm going to spread my wings a little, Mom. Where else could I be this safe? You don't let me go anywhere in this world. Please, Mom?" Micah softened her attitude.

We had been detoured off the whole Jet talk. I wanted some answers so that I could feel okay about it.

I stared at Micah. She was beautiful, and she'd never gone against my wishes before. Had Tristan and I instilled enough in her if anything happened? Had she been taught to fight for her life if she needed to? Defend her body, choose the right? A knock at the door interrupted my thoughts.

"Micah?" It was Jet. "We have to go. They're waiting on only you."

Micah's face scrunched, and she brought her hands together as she begged. "Please, Mom. Dad is fine with it."

"Micah?" Jet banged on the door again.

"Coming!" Micah hollered back, looking over at the door as she spoke.

"Right, Mom?" She moved her gaze back from the door to meet mine.

All I could do was to nod once. Micah ran at me, hugged me, and kissed my cheek. She had almost made it out the door. "Micah, wait!" She turned and looked at me, confused. I took the necklace from around my neck as I walked toward her.

"This was given to me by someone important. Let it guide you and keep you safe," I told Micah as I placed the beautiful necklace Marissa had given me at the kiosk around her neck. Perhaps she didn't know the story or the meaning surrounding it, but it made me feel somewhat better about her leaving if she had it. However, the dreadful ache in my gut wouldn't subside.

"I love it, Mom," she whispered, and then she was gone.

I don't know how long I stood there. My girl was gone, and it didn't sit right with me, no matter what angle I looked at it. I couldn't do anything about it, and I couldn't argue anymore about it. She was gone from the palace for her first experience without me.

Sitting on the couch, I questioned and wondered if I brewed up these ideas. With Micah gone, was I overthinking everything? Was my mind playing tricks on me? Jet, where was he in this picture?

Moving to the window, I looked over the white winter grounds beneath the window. I tried to think of my parents and my adoptive parents and what they would do. And you know what I came up with? Zero. I had nothing. I longed for parents who weren't there in either life.

I hadn't heard Tristan come in, "Hey." he said, wrapping me up in his arms.

"Hey." I softly replied.

Tristan held me like that with my back to him for some time.

Tristan gently hugged me more; then, he spoke the words I couldn't agree with at all. "It's okay, Jade. Micah will be fine."

Rather than arguing, I sighed and shrugged my shoulders. He couldn't see my face, and for that, I was thankful. He was an amazing man and had been for all our lives together. So why couldn't I accept his words?

"I think we need to get out tonight and run wild, Jade. It had been a long time since just he and I had gone out. It's been a long time." Sighing, I nodded, approving his request.

"Maybe we can stir up some magic in the world, and the Higher Powers will feel its time again." He trailed off.

How many times had I heard him say that before? I had lost count. Why we hadn't been blessed again, I didn't know? I yearned for a son as much as Tristan.

"Yes. Perhaps a little magic is in the air tonight." He wanted to take my mind off Micah, I knew, but being blessed again would be amazing.

Chapter Eleven

Mary

Buddy (Kade) sat looking at me with sad eyes, as usual. The necklace had been missing ever since Grant's last visit. It did all of us no good without it. It has undoubtedly been a life-power in more ways than one.

The last several weeks had turned into the most brutal weeks of my entire existence. My spells and ritual books were less than helpful. That necklace served as a lifeline to the Higher Powers, and now it had been removed from our possession. The best answers I could get from Kade were whining and head nods.

"Mary?" Mandy stood next to me in the kitchen as we prepared lunch together. "Is it bad that I feel so… oh, I don't know, defeated?"

"You can't give up." Then, grabbing Mandy's arm, I looked her straight in the eyes. "You never give up! That's when evil wins, Mandy. You know that!"

Mandy sighed and shook her head. "This isn't right, Mary. I feel like I'm losing you." Ah-ha, the heart of the matter.

"We all have to go rest sometime, Mandy. I have been a tool for centuries. Even I need to rest and walk in the light of our Higher Powers." I tried to smile, hoping to comfort her. Instead, I saw the tears brimming.

Mandy took my hands in hers. "What will I do? This life means nothing without you here."

"Nonsense! Quit feeling sorry for yourself! You have yet to have a life filled with joy other than taking care of me." It was gentle but honest. "Lord! I'm not gone yet. Not even close! Just because I show signs of aging doesn't mean I'm leaving tomorrow. Now, enough of this chatter. We have a race to save!"

"Kade… Buddy… I still don't know what to call you." The dog growled back with irritation. "Well, you should've kept a closer watch on that darn necklace. You're supposed to be a watchdog still, too!" I meant it as a joke, but he took it rather seriously and left the room with his tail between his legs.

"Kade… wait! I meant nothing by that. We've got this. Come back here." But he didn't.

Mandy and I finished lunch and put Kade's sandwich in his bowl. Eventually, I hoped he would get hungry enough to come back and eat it and forgive me as well.

"Should we go to the office now and work, Mary?" Mandy finished putting the last dish away.

"Yes, I think we should. I need to stop going over the same steps that will not change. I'm missing something, and I think I had a brilliant idea."

"Amen!" Mandy clapped her hands together happily. "I'll go find Kade and meet you there. He can't go without lunch."

"Okay. See you shortly." I whirled the new ideas around in my head. It wasn't a lot to go on, but it was something.

* * *

The banging on my door in the middle of the night wasn't a common occurrence. I hadn't been okay in weeks and Kade hadn't returned. Both Mandy and I had cried ourselves dry. Mandy tried to comfort me from my guilt. I meant nothing by the comment I'd made to Kade about being a better watchdog over the one object that gave him authentic life. As you do with items that get used more and more, we had all been careless with it. Kade couldn't have used it much more anyway, as it had sucked so much of my life away already. On the alternate side, though, having it gone had now taken the exact toll. I couldn't win. The cards were stacked against me, pushing me to race time and figure all this out. Even the journals Amy and Jet had been using all these years stopped transmitting altogether. Either that or they had stopped using them. I figured I wasn't receiving them with how I felt and the tiny spark of power left in me.

"Coming!" I hollered as I put my night robe on. I slowly got out of bed, and my blood pumped fast at being startled from my slumber.

"Mary?" It was Tristan!

"Mom?" And Grant!

"Yes! Yes, I'm coming." They both had keys and had let themselves in. I was unprepared to see all of them there, though, except....

"Where is Jet?" I skimmed the room a second and third time.

"Mom?" Grant came over to give me a soft hug. "What has happened to you?"

"I'm aging, you, doof," I replied lightly, still looking for Jet.

"Kade!" The dog came around the side of Nonny, where Amethyst also stood.

"Kade? Who's Kade? Mom, are you okay?" Grant's voice amped with concern.

"Shadow Night Kade, Jade's brother. Now, where's Jet, and why are you all here?"

"That makes little sense at all." Grant was stuck on me, calling the dog Kade. "That's Buddy, and we found him one day while we were riding in my Hummer, on our way here. Which I know makes no sense at all. But calling him Kade? That's ridiculous."

"We just figured it was fate with Grant and Buddy." Tristan came up to me as well and hugged me. Everyone hugged me.

"Wow, it's Kade?" Jade had gone down on her knees in front of the dog. They were eye to eye. "Tell me more, Mary?" Jade pleaded. She wanted somehow to believe it could be true, and that Buddy was her brother Kade.

"It was the necklace, Higher Powers, whoever is in charge of this parade. But your necklace was the key, and then it disappeared the last time Grant was here."

"Micah has it. I hope, still…." Jade quietly stated looking at Buddy in disbelief. "Grant brought it back last time he had been here and found it on the floor."

"Well, that necklace has a purpose still." I nodded. Grant looked sick at what I had called him out on.

"I didn't know." His voice rifled with guilt.

"I know, and perhaps we should've said something. But we had all agreed to keep it between us in case there were extra eyes on us here. We didn't know who to trust." I explained.

"Your son would've been a nice start to whom to confide in," Grant said with irritation.

"There's too much going on. I have a good idea why you're here and why Jet isn't here." I had enough of the debate. The necklace wasn't here, so why discuss it any further?

"And Micah," Jade added.

"But Amy's here?" I looked around for answers.

"Yes, I didn't want to stay. They're not right. I had to escape." Amy's voice flattened.

"Drobny?" I questioned.

They all nodded.

"We came here, thinking you might help. But, seeing you like this…." Grant left the rest of the statement off.

"I'm old now. Not dead. And even though I don't know what is going on, I can assure you I'm quite current on many things going on with the children. At least with Jet and Amy."

"What do you mean?" Amy asked.

"Your journals were meant for my eyes to see. Whatever you put in there, I saw." Amy's eyes grew wide. "You have nothing to be embarrassed about. I had to figure out some way to watch over you. The first protection and binding I did, didn't work out so well."

"Grant? Why are you all here after the way you practically ran me off and treated me so poorly?" I had to admit I couldn't believe them all being here still.

Grant's demeanor changed. "Yeah, about that. The Drobny have their ways."

"They couldn't have done anything without Kiryana, though. She was our weak link. So, the palace became poisoned with them. It was after Amy escaped and came back to let us know what was going on."

"With the Drobny?" I asked again.

No one answered me right off the bat. "Oh yes, with Keegan and Diamonté." I knew it!

"How did you know?" Jade had stood up, placing her hand on top of Kade's head.

"Journal entries. I didn't know what to do. And then Kade came into the light, and my health started going wrong, and then the necklace and Kade both disappeared."

"Were you planning on letting us know?" Grant asked.

"Well, yes. But I haven't seen you for a while. It isn't like I can jump in a car and fly on up there. You're here now, and that matters." I patted his arm. The tension in the room increased.

"Now… Jet." I looked at Amy.

"They released him, Grandmamma." My worst fear had been revealed.

"I knew it…." I whispered back.

"Can you release me, Grandmamma? I know I can help." Amy came to my side. Kade left Jade's side and came up next to her.

"You know this dog, or Kade, however you want to look at him, has been your protector all this time," I told her and also looked at the others.

Amy glanced down, and as if seeing the animal for the first time, she smiled. "I see him, Grandmamma."

Well, that was a shocker!

"What do you mean, Amy? You see my brother?" Jade stood at her side now.

"Kind of like that, but kind of not like that. She is telling you the truth, though. He is there." Amy explained, and I nodded in agreement.

"And Micah's with Jet, still?" I asked Amy in particular.

"Yes." Again, her voice flat.

I pondered that. "Is it another Nonny and Grant type case?" Tristan asked me.

I shrugged, as I didn't know. "Could be. It could be the Drobny. Keegan and Diamonté are involved, so who knows."

"She had taken off the necklace while we were there. It called to me, and she hadn't wanted it. So I took it. I have it here." Amy didn't look at Jade or Tristan.

"You stole it from her and then kept it to yourself?" Jade shrieked at Amy. Nonny and Grant both came to Amy's side, pulling her next to them for safety.

"How dare you take that, Amy! So now she has no protection!" Jade and Tristan both stood to one side in outrage as my family stood on the other side.

"It wouldn't have helped." Amy defended herself. "She took it off as soon as we got to the Drobny place. Jet told her he didn't like it, and it made her look ugly."

Jade looked as if she was about to explode, with Tristan right behind her. Kade… Buddy, Kade whined and came to the middle of the gap between them and in front of me. He barked when the commotion and arguing wouldn't stop.

It silenced the room. Crouching down in front of him, I spoke softly so the room would remain quiet if they wanted to hear what I had to say.

"Amy, give me the necklace, please." I held my hand out as she dug for the necklace in her pocket.

"It called to me, Grandmamma." Amy cried as she placed the necklace into the palm of my hand.

"You're fine, Amy," I told her while looking at Jade. She was fired up, alright.

"That's all Micah had. How can you say that? Amy, you betrayed us, and now look at where we are!" Mama bear was all out now. It needed to be stopped before words went too far and couldn't be taken back.

"Jade, you do not know what you're talking about; you think you know how everything works now? Well, I assure you… you don't! So, calm down, and I can probably explain some of this." I had to hurry before Jade said anything more than she might regret.

Jade folded her arms in front of her as Tristan kept his arms around her waist. "I'm listening, but you'd better be quick. I guarantee I don't see it the way you do."

"Good lord, child. What has gotten into you?" This was a side of Jade I hadn't ever seen. "Do you not remember anything from the day I gave you that necklace?"

"I remember it very well, Mary. I'm sorry if you think I'm not fair right now, but my child's life is undeniably in danger because of Amy's brother."

"He is part of your blood, too. Do not forget that. This necklace served its purpose for you and Tristan. But it also belongs to the Shadow Night and the powers that made it. Micah took it off."

"Because Jet told her to!" Jade interrupted.

"Jade, if Micah were supposed to have that necklace, I promise you, she would still have it. There are so many hands working right now on bringing peace and balance to the entire universe." I shook my head because even I couldn't believe it. "You would truly be in awe if you knew."

"Like whom? Because all I see is darkness everywhere. Even my clansmen have been put under some shitty spell! Tell me, how could the Higher Powers allow that after everything we have been through?"

"Things fall into place, like the necklace into their destiny. Stop for one moment and think about the timing of everything. Even I've been hard at work with Mandy and Kade, and until recently, we were on a path. Now, not so much. But all of you here with the necklace. I know we're all here for a purpose. Micah is strong, and she will be okay. Believe that, Jade, Tristan, all of you're a part of a wonderful destiny." Suppose I could restore even a little faith into the room right now because it was very much needed!

They all stood there, staring at me. Even Amy had silenced her tears. "Now, Kade, you need to talk to your sister." The dog stepped back, not afraid, of course, but knowing my condition. I knew he didn't want to until he had a real purpose to serve.

"Kade, I'll be okay. I'm becoming crotchety and demanding in my old age. It isn't time until I say it's time. Just for a quick spell. Come on." Kade cocked his head like he listened to someone for a moment and then came to me.

"Now, before I do this… while I said I'm practically an ox, it is taking quite a toll on me. But, whatever the balance is, the necklace seems to energize more as I deteriorate. So let's speak our piece, and Kade can let us know if there's anything more. we need to know, Okay?" They all continued to stare at me like I had lost my marbles. "Still non-believers, I see."

"My brother is not a dog," Jade said. Kade growled at her. I initially guessed an apology would come up in Jade's near future. Only minutes ago, she believed in Kade being Buddy. What… was going on?!

Kneeling, I wrapped and clasped the necklace quickly. In the blink of an eye, Kade stood before us. Again, I thanked all the Higher Powers for having included clothing in the spell for him.

"Kade?" Jade said with much hesitation.

"It is me, Jade," he replied.

"But how?" She drifted to be utterly shocked.

"Same way with you, I suppose. We all have a purpose, no matter what form we take. We all matter. What doesn't kill us strengthens us? Stronger? You know that." Kade tried to kid around, but it was a profound moment.

Jade wasted no more time embracing her brother as she sobbed. "You've been here all this time, and I didn't know. How could I not have known? What good is being a queen with amazing gifts and not knowing something like this?"

"It wasn't exactly like that. And I haven't always been this way. But Mary is correct. We need to keep this brief." Kade looked at me. My hand tingled, but I didn't tell him anything with my eyes. This was important.

Tristan came over and shook Kade's hand. "It's been a long time. I, ahh… I'm sorry if I ever treated you poorly over the years. I know I gave Grant some shit about having you."

"You're fine, Tristan. I can hardly blame you, knowing our kind rarely get along with dogs. They had a lot of faith in Grant." Kade nodded toward Grant.

"Hey." Grant greeted him and also thought back on history spending with someone he thought was a dog.

"Same goes for you. Don't worry; you were always good to me," Kade chuckled.

"That's good because I was wracking my brain trying to be sure." They clasped hands. I could see Kade was eager to talk to one girl in particular.

"Amy." Kade shook her hand but held it. She looked back at him with no look of disbelief or surprise or anything that the others had shown.

"It is so nice finally to meet the sweet young lady who has been shielded in my heart ever since Mary placed the binding and protection spell on you. My life became complete when she did that. It's been my pleasure guarding you all this time. I only wished I could've done a better job for your brother, Jet." Kade seemed more angelic than he had ever appeared before.

"He's in trouble," Amy said to him.

"I know." Kade's look saddened.

"I can't feel him anymore," Amy confessed.

"Me either, Amy. Me either." Kade shook his head sadly.

"Do you know why?" Jade asked Kade.

My other hand tingled. I wasn't sure how much longer I could keep the blank look on my face. Although, maybe no one would notice my distress, anyway. It wasn't like I was being watched right now.

"What I can tell you, Jade, is everything Amy has said is very much correct. You can't be upset with her. Keegan and Diamanté will have their way. I'm no closer to knowing why they're even still around than you're."

"Sorry, Amy," Jade told her.

"It's okay. I understand." Bless her!

A cough escaped me. I don't know even where it came from, but Kade took it seriously. "I need to tell you all a couple of things quickly. First, Mary is getting weaker by the minute, with me here."

"Nonsense." I tried blowing it off. "I'm still fine."

"Mom, you told us it needed to be quick." Grant came to my side.

"Well, this is important, and we're wasting time. Go ahead, Kade." I nodded and encouraged him to continue while smiling up at Grant. He scowled back.

Kade returned his gaze to Amy. "Nonny and Grant, I need to unbind Amy. Her destiny has been unfolded."

"What? No! I can't lose her." Nonny didn't quite understand the concept of everything, but didn't like what she heard.

"No, Mom. It's okay. Kade's right. They have released Jet." Amy sounded much older than she appeared. My grandbaby was growing up.

"At least if Mary releases her, it will be with the light of Shadow Night," Kade said as he motioned to me.

"I don't know if I can, though. Kade, you know how powerless I have become." My legs were numbing, and I could feel the tingling turning to pain. I must have looked like a wreck.

"Mary, push past the pain. Look to the light and see the rays of the Higher Powers and the Oracle inside. Believe, and Amy will help you." Kade's voice again seemed to be filled with angels speaking.

"I will?" Amy, for the first time that evening, seemed surprised.

"Yes, Amy, you will. Now help me with this necklace, Amy. Wear it for me and keep it safe."

Amy nodded and unclasped the lock. Kade was gone, and a dog sat at her feet.

"Amazing," Amy muttered.

Everyone muttered in agreement as well. All I wanted to do was lay down and close my eyes for a bit. The pain had subsided in my hands and legs, but a dull ache remained. I moved from beside Grant to the nearest chair.

"Oh, Mary." Nonny remained at my side. "It's like you've aged ten years right in front of our eyes."

I couldn't even force a smile or deny what she said.

"I'm so sorry, everyone…." Jade's tone had mellowed. "It's just that, well, you know what I have been through with Keegan before, and I'm concerned as a mother. Micah is all we have right now who is full-blooded Royal. And I don't mean that to sound anything less for Amy and Jet. But, oh, damn, I'm making more of a mess of things." Jade sat down and put her face in her hands.

Tristan sat down next to her. "Our daughter is amazing and well-trained. They have no power over her. We're her parents, Jade. She would never hurt us."

Jade lifted her face out of her hands and stared at Tristan. "Yeah, well, I hope you're right in all that you say and think."

Tristan moved to comfort her more, but she abruptly stood up and left.

"Leave her," I told him meekly. "Give her some space, for now, Tristan. Her head is muddled with information, old and new." He didn't need to know about the possible affair of Jade and Keegan when she didn't even know what was real and what was fake herself. Of course, or real, but this night wasn't the night for pillow talk.

Tristan sat back down, still unsure whether he should listen to me. He ran his hand through his hair impatiently. "I'll wait for a bit. But, if she doesn't calm down and come back, I'll go after her," he stated firmly.

I nodded in agreement, as that seemed fair. "I need some time. Just a little time, and then I'll work with Amy." Grant and Nonny nodded.

"Here, Mom, let me help you to your room." Grant put his arm around me and helped me up.

"Thank you. That sounds like heaven." But, boy, did it ever.

"I can help, too." Amy came to my other side, and with her touch, I felt peace.

"That feels lovely, Amy. Thank you."

She looked at me funny but continued helping. "I love you, Grandmamma." She kissed my cheek.

"And Grandmamma loves you," I said before yawning long and loud. "Goodness, I'm beat."

Chapter Twelve

Mary

Getting a plan together takes time when dealing with the devil. Or, in this case, Keegan and my old nemesis, Diamonté. Why evil bastards are so hard to kill and easy to bring back is not right. And on that thought, had Keegan been brought back from some sort of dead state?

Each day, I traveled down my staircase of death further and further. The landing was getting closer and closer. It was as if I were the hourglass, and once it was empty, then what?

Several days later, I was surprised to be called to in a dream, and even it was much different this time. I was young and vibrant as I had been when I had first met Diamonté.

"I was wondering if you would ever bring me back here. I'm at a loss at what to do." I tried explaining myself to the smoke people's Chief. "How is it evil can keep prevailing over the life of Shadow Night and in so many forms?" This time, I waited for the Chief to speak.

"Evil. Yes. Everywhere. Form and shape-shift, yes. Disguised so innocent will accept it. You see, for evil to exist, it manipulate spirit. Like medicine, it becomes nonworking. It must find a new disguise." A woman came to his side as he finished. She was young but looked wise.

Her English was much better, and she spoke without fragments, which surprised me, "It's time for you to go on your quest."

Perplexed, I asked, "Am I dead?"

She smiled and shook her head.

"Phew!" My heartbeat doubled; I swear!

"Is that why I'm young again? For this quest?" She nodded. "What's the quest for? And why now? Why not way back when?"

She chuckled, "Because He has a plan, and just when you think you have figured out the plan… maybe you haven't. Marissa, you have been through a lot, and for that, we are all incredibly grateful for your success. But this quest that you must venture on now; well, don't you see your life has been leading you to this very moment?"

"No… not at all. I have been through hell too many times. It's been a replay; God only knows how many times." I knew the tone of my voice was sarcastic, but what did they want with me now?

"Five." She held up her hand.

"Well, I'm glad I don't remember them all. I can't take much more of this, and now you have made me young again. I can handle the getting old and passing away peacefully simply fine, but please don't make me go through life again with that bastard Diamonté." I pleaded.

"You won't. At least, I don't think you will. You're on a life path, and it isn't supposed to be about Diamonté. Unless you change that." The woman looked deeply into my eyes. "Are you afraid?"

"Well, yes! Of course, I'm! But, I still don't know what this is all about or why this time has changed so drastically. Can you tell me that?" My voice sounded shrill.

"Amethyst." It was the only clue she gave me. She looked at the Chief and bowed before leaving.

"Amethyst? The change in the universe is her?" I asked the Chief now since the woman had left.

He nodded. "Yes. She lived."

"And what about Jet?" Would I have to worry about him dying or becoming like his grandfather?

"Don't know." He pointed his pipe and shook it at me. "Change is to come. All things come to an end."

Here we go again. The Chief and his chopped-up rhyming English. "Life?"

"For some." He answered.

"But not all?"

"We see." Raising his eyebrows at me, he shook his head.

"So, if I fail at knowing what I'm supposed to do here as the typical heroine, who does it affect?"

The woman appeared again. Thank goodness!

"There are a few things you'll need and also need to know." She had a few more women standing behind her, holding various items. I waited as she turned around and took the first item from the hands of one of those waiting.

She turned around and placed a small dove into my hands, of all things. It didn't fly off immediately. "What? A bird?"

"When you need wings. She will be there." Then the dove flew out of my hands and into the night. The fire crackled loudly behind her like fireworks. I watched all the women and the Chief as they raised their hands when the bird took flight.

"Ciantaramo," the Chief roared. All the women repeated it.

"What's that?" I asked the woman I was speaking with, "What does that mean?"

"That is the name you'll call out for her. You'll remember when the time is right. Have faith." She smiled warmly.

"Ciantaramo? I'll remember it. Are you sure? And I'll know when to use the word? Is it during this quest I need her, or later, or what?" The questions spiraled out of my mouth. My heart raced.

"You know." The Chief reiterated what the woman already had told me.

"I hope you're right. What else are you going to give me to save the world and not explain to me?" Sarcasm again oozed from me. Having my youth again brought back the fighting spirit I hadn't felt in years. I knew they meant well, but why did everything have to be so complicated? If my accomplishments mattered so much, why make it so difficult for me to achieve them?

"He said to tell you that there's only burden where you choose to have burden. We all have a purpose; only some come with more responsibility. You have earned this right because with each damnation of Diamonté. You have succeeded."

"I have?" That was news to me.

"Diamanté chose you. He powerfully regrets it but cannot control himself. You know that. You have been touched."

"And no one else has been 'touched?'" I couldn't believe that. "What about between Grant and Nonny, then?"

"Good and evil. You know this, Marissa. Diamonté, when he touched you, had been to another side of damnation. But it is rectifiable finally. There's a chance for real peace. So many will succumb to their worst fears. Jade lived, and another door opened to keep this destiny forever. But through those same doors, shadows came too. Too much dark keeps the universe unbalanced. Through you, the grace will be found." She turned to another woman and took a small object from her hands.

"While you dwindle in the limbo of life. Drink this before you leave with the others to rule your destiny now." As she placed the vial in my hands, I saw red liquid within it.

"It doesn't look very appetizing." I cringed inside at the thought of drinking it. "Blood?" Looking up again, I asked the woman.

"Perhaps." And, of course, she smiled again.

"You want me to drink the blood of what before I go to the Drobny lair?"

"It will cloak you." She answered what she wanted to.

"An answer. A first for me here!" Well, that was exciting.

"From Diamonté, I'm assuming?" A slight nod, but another answer. I hated that vampire, and having to say his name repeatedly was nasty!

“There’s one more thing I must give you. Please try to keep an open mind.” She turned to the last woman remaining.

“Here. Do not unwrap this until Diamonté knows you’re there. We’ll know nothing from the time you leave here until you unwrap this.” There was a look of concern on her face now. Or was it fear?

“Until he has a visual on me or what? Will it bring you all or take him out or what?” So I had to carry and conceal all this stuff and remember to call for wings when I needed it. And they called it a quest. I called it a hot mess.

“I wish I had never met Diamonté,” I whispered under my breath.

“Do not say such words. You graced by God. Where faith now?” The Chief looked downright saddened by my small admission. He walked away and stood behind the fire.

“He said to tell you, if not you, then who, and perhaps we all would not be here. It is your path and destiny, and you need to accept it.”

“I have. But it doesn’t make it any easier. I know where I’m in life. I’m not afraid. I’m regretful for not having a normal human life. The ‘why me?’ will always be there. Doesn’t every superhero wonder how they came to be?” I tried to smile at my example of being a superhero. But, unfortunately, my superpowers were about drained.

“He was your fate, just as everyone around you is, as well. The table has been set.”

“For what? A massacre all over again? What if I refuse? I cannot bear to see my family die.” That was a thought that haunted me often. All the ‘what ifs,’ if I did this, and not that. Who would it affect?

“Your quest starts here and now. Your destiny is there and later.” She ended with a typical smoke people rhyme.

“Perfect. Which way to pass go?” My life had turned into a game.

* * *

I wasn’t back at my house, and I wasn’t surrounded by the smoke people any longer. I didn’t know where I was in actuality. Earthbound, moon-bound, dimension-bound. It wasn’t dark, but it certainly wasn’t light. It felt like I was alone.

"I guess I should've asked how long this quest was supposed to take. It sure isn't helping me save any kids." I muttered conversation to myself as I trudged along. I did not know what to do other than walk.

I must have walked five miles before coming across a sign that had three ways for me to go.

"What the heck is this? A choose your ending quest?" But, of course, no one was there to answer my question.

"Let's see. If I go to the left, I go with the sign that reads Amethyst. To the right is Jet, and if I continue on the same path, I go with Micah." So why would Micah be on there? Well, why not, I guess.

"The smoke woman told me this was a quest about Amethyst. So, I'm assuming I should go left on that path." I looked as far down each path as my eyesight would take me. They all looked the same; dark, deserted paths. Period.

"But, what if that's not the case, and I should already know what is with Amethyst, or it will be revealed? Hmm. Decisions." Once again, I looked down each path, hoping to see a sign of something new.

"Amethyst, though, is the only one I can locate. The other two are together. Maybe knowing more about one of them will help me later. But what if Amethyst needs to know something now?" My mind was spinning, and I didn't know what path to take.

"Who do I need to know about now?" The decision finally unraveled and became apparent. "Amethyst." Without another glance down the other two choices, I headed down the path with my granddaughter's name.

After some time, I saw birds flying overhead. Some looked like the dove that I had held earlier in my hand. There were vultures, eagles, hawks, and more than I could identify.

"What do you all want?" Could it be a sign to use wings?

"Nah." I kept walking. I could finally see some sort of buildings coming up. Getting closer and closer, I recognized the place. Though it was now old and deserted, it was the place Diamonté and I had first met.

"What is this? A trip down memory lane?" I wondered how it could've anything to do with Amethyst.

Of course, I knew where my home had been, but that hadn't been where Diamonté and I had first met. I walked down the middle of the dirt road between structures that still stood, just as they had so many centuries before. Made from mud and wood, they should've been long gone, or at the very least, in partial ruins.

My home was one of several on the other side of the outskirts of the town. I walked until my shoes were at the very edge of the pathway leading to the wooden door that hinged on the mud sidings. It had never gotten frigid here, so the windows that had been cut into the mud only had a cloth over them, blowing in the wind ever so gently.

The feeling was calm and welcoming. I wondered if my items were still inside, as the rest of the town seemed to have been untouched. It was as if I had only left there the day prior.

"Yes. Everything looks the same," I whispered as I thought about my history here. Touching furniture and kitchenware, I walked through the small rooms. Nothing stood out within these walls. Perhaps the place Diamonté and I met was where I needed to go.

Exiting the house, I ventured out back and began the short walk to the River in the Desert, as it had been called when I had lived there. It was a free-flowing stream that flowed all year long, supplying us with all the water we needed for animals, crops, and personal use.

Bending down, I put my hand into the strong current of the stream that still ran freely and scooped up water that I drank thirstily. There was a place upstream I still had to visit, hoping the rocks still stuck out of the water far enough to cross.

I finally got close enough that I could see them. "Thank goodness, Mary. The water is as frosty as I remembered."

Carefully, I stepped on each one, thanking the smoke people for my youth for this quest. In my natural physical state, there was no way I could've crossed those safely. I would've fallen and been swept away, long gone.

This side of the stream held the desert with a deep thicket of tumbleweed and cactus. After a short walk near to where Diamonté had found me, I choked on my breath.

"No… no… no, no." I backed away in disbelief. I didn't want to go any further. Grave markers sat in formation a few feet in front of me. It was a clearing for the dead -- Diamonté's work, his headcount. I wanted to throw up. I needed to cry.

Kneeling and putting my head into my hands, I couldn't believe what I had found. I didn't want to see the cemetery of the babies who I had once carried inside me. It was all too much, and I couldn't hold the emotions back anymore. I sobbed for the lives he'd taken in his haste, the children who didn't get to experience life but succumbed to his hands of death.

It was a while before I could stand without collapsing. My heart hurt with so much pain for my babies. I walked forward, saying a silent prayer for each. There were more than I could remember. Were the smoke people sure there were only five cycles? Had Diamonté been hell-bent on thinking he could change the outcome? I fully understood their term of being touched by Diamonté. It was everlasting.

"It will end!" I screamed out for my children.

The last grave was unmarked and different from the others. It was almost separated from the rest, and the dirt remained to the side. Yet, somehow. I knew he meant it for Amethyst.

In outrage, I pulled the stone to where he tried to mark her and threw it. His symbolism disgusted me. "Never! You bastard! Never will you get your final grave filled!" Kicking the dirt back into the hole, I worked and cussed that horrible bastard out!

I didn't stop until the hole was filled and no trace of any kind of marked area was left. "What has this got to do with anything now?" I screamed. My voice echoed around me everywhere.

"This is a shitty quest!" I yelled. "How dare you bring me here!" They had brought me here, right? True, it had been my choice also, but it had been the likely choice. The Higher Powers had to have known I would choose Amethyst. Right?

Now what? Stay here? Is this what they wanted me to see? I already knew Amethyst was something special. I needed to leave this area. Diamonté had made the site of our first meeting, and a place of doom greeted me there. Perfect and so fitting.

Walking back to my house seemed reasonable. Finally, I could collect my thoughts and perhaps put something of this mess together. At least I could hope to do that.

I went inside and laid down on my bed of straw. It wasn't the most comfortable thing now that I knew how it felt to sleep in a proper bed. It was, in fact, excessively uncomfortable, but I continued attempting to find a comfortable spot in it.

"Ow!" Straw could be poky, but not like that. Sitting up, I turned around and felt where the poke came from as a purple gleam caught my eyes.

"Amethyst?" Several pieces of amethyst were under the straw, and I dug them all out until I was sure no more were hidden there.

"Now, what does that mean?" I pondered that question as I carried them to the table and set them all down, taking a seat on a chair.

Studying each of them, I didn't know how long the noise outside had been building. Horse hooves were trampling closer.

"Shit!" I wanted to look outside to see who it was. It had been so quiet this whole time, and now my heart felt like it was beating in my throat.

"Stop!" a voice hissed. I recognized Keegan's deranged dialect. Everything he did seemed to echo in my house. His sniff of the air sounded like he sat next to me.

"Smell that?" I didn't know or care who he asked. I wanted them to get moving. I had stayed too long, not considering that this place was still in use, considering that open grave. Hindsight. All hindsight.

I kept quiet and tried to still my thunderous, beating heart.

I heard several more sniffs of the air before another thing spoke. I didn't know what to call them anymore. 'Things' seemed about right!

"Human?" he answered Keegan.

"Couldn't be. But that's what I thought I smelled as well."

Shit! They could smell me. Thinking about nothing other than what was happening, I opened and drank just a little of the red vial. It couldn't hurt to have a little now and save the rest for Diamonté, I hoped, later. I wouldn't have a later if I didn't do something now.

And then I felt it stop. My heart stopped cold in my chest, but I was still alive.

"It's gone." The things outside all agreed.

"Yes, but something has been here. Let's go find it!" With that comment, the 'things' and their horses ran off.

I wasn't sure how long I had, but I scooped up the amethysts and ran out of there in the opposite direction. My heart beat again, and it filled me with excruciating pain. I needed to be quiet, but I couldn't stop the screaming.

"Grandmamma! Wake up!" I heard Amy's voice through my pain. Opening my eyes, I looked into her eyes and saw I was back in my bed.

"Grandmamma?" Amy frowned. "What happened? Are you okay?"

I nodded, looking around her head at Grant's upset face. "How long has it been?"

"You've been out of it for almost a week," Grant told me. "Like in a coma or something."

I was in shock! Throwing the covers back, I weakly moved as fast as I could. We had work to do!

"What are those?" Then, under the sheets, they saw the pouches the smoke people had given me.

"Mine." Scooping them up, I headed for my office.

"Let's get to work," I said over my shoulder.

Grant and Tristan were on my heels. "Jade's pregnant."

I stopped in my tracks. Oh, the timing!

Chapter Thirteen

Mary

I couldn't focus on the tedious tasks I was expected to perform until checking on Jade. So much time had passed between her pregnancies. Even I had wondered how they were expected to carry on the Royal name with just Micah. "Where is she?"

"Out on the couch watching TV," Tristan told me, waiting to see if I would head back the other way to where Jade was or continue into my office or study. Whatever I called it that day, multi-use room now, for magic or spells, and keeping grandchildren and myself alive-type room.

When I moved in the opposite direction, he and Grant quickly adjusted and moved ahead of me to the TV room.

Jade lay on her side on the couch, chatting with Nonny and Mandy. Nonny spoke first. "We heard the commotion, and Amy filled us in." Then Nonny gestured to her daughter, who walked from the kitchen with a glass of water.

"I thought you might be thirsty." Amy brought the glass to me.

Her quick insight surprised me. "Parched. Thank you, Amy." I took the glass and sat down slowly at Jade's feet.

“How are you, Jade?” I gazed at her.

“Good. The same as last time.” She spoke before attempting to stop a dry heave from starting again.

“How long have you been like this?” I asked her.

Mandy spoke up before Jade could. “Just a few days,” she blurted out.

“Three?” I again tried to talk to Jade and get confirmation.

Jade nodded. “Yes, Mandy’s correct. Ironically, I stood in the kitchen watching Mandy and Amy make lunch. There must be something about that kitchen.” She tried to joke, but the poor thing looked horrible. “Sorry.” She apologized like it had been her fault to get pregnant at such a time of impasse.

“Nonsense. Babies bring joy. Jade, I think it’s a good omen. And trust me, with what I saw in my nightmares. Well… that wasn’t a nightmare. That was a bad omen!” Looking around, I announced, “I’ll fill you all in when we go back to get started on a few things.”

Grant and Tristan nodded. “What about Jade?” Tristan wondered.

“What about her? We do everything according to plan and hope that we make it to our destination in time to handle what needs to be handled. I don’t want to deliver the baby with her outside of the palace any more than you. But we’ll do whatever we need to do.” I wanted to sound confident. I hoped I had.

“You think there’s that chance?” Jade asked meekly.

“I think we’re safe. I’m ninety-nine percent sure you’ll be fine and still pregnant when you return to the palace, but time is of the essence. Getting you there will be the first battle at hand. When the Elders and clan members see you, that will be a whole new battle. I have faith in you, Jade. Higher Powers don’t give us any more than we can handle. You know that. The Higher Powers have blessed you, and that is utterly amazing. A gift.” Jade had tried to sit up as much as possible during our conversation. But being a pregnant vampire was a whole different ballgame than being pregnant as a human. It was their weakest state, after all.

“I’ll soldier up,” Jade assured all of us.

“You’ll be fine. I just know it.” Amy hugged Jade, then looked at her aunt like she never looked at her before. There was something there.

"Amy." I broke the silence that had fallen over the room. Then, standing up, I walked to the center of the room.

"Yes, Grandmamma?" Amy stood up like a soldier waiting for her orders.

"It's time," I stated the one fact.

"It's way past the time, Grandmamma." Amy moved past me, touching my arm, before heading back to the multi-task room.

I still had the pouches clenched in my hands. I didn't need them right now, but soon I would. Yes, too soon, I would.

I also turned and headed back to the multi-purpose room, with Tristan and Grant on my tail.

* * *

I called to him in his dog form. "Kade, come over here next to Amy, in this circle." I made the circle using the same items I had used the night the twins were born.

"Perfect." It delighted me with how things were going. I had placed the pouches from the smoke people on my desk. Grant had fidgeted and pushed on them a few times until I had to step in and scold him like a child. After that, he was next to them again.

"Just leave them alone, Grant." I was tired, and his childlike behavior didn't help.

"I know who you got them from." He touched one.

"Grant! Quit. Please focus on your daughter! We are doing something massive here, and you keep playing with those bags. Yes! Yes, the smoke people gave them to me." Grant finally seemed to snap out of it and looked at his daughter sheepishly.

A short knock on the door interrupted us. "Jade was wondering if she needed to come back yet," Mandy asked from the other side of the door.

"No, I won't need her. But you can tell Nonny she needs to come back here. Even though she wasn't there for Jet's release, I want her here for Amy's. It's important for our turn of events." Well, it would seem appropriate. I was kind of flying by the seat of my pants here, after all. Of course, I didn't want them to know that.

I was pretty much powerless, but I had an inkling that there would be a changing of the guard once I got going.

Nonny opened the door and walked in. Then, smiling at her daughter, she went over and stood next to Grant. He took her hand, and they looked lovingly at each other. Just that brief flicker of love seemed to spark the room.

"Now, the necklace. I had created another one when I had my bright idea, what seemed eons ago. I laid them side by side on the desk. They looked nothing alike. One was enchantingly and more beautiful than the other. My homemade one looked like something made during a shop class, but that was okay. My handmade necklace of three colored metal pieces hung on a gold chain.

"I know what these represent." So, I was telling Kade, in particular, reading his cocked head after I held them up for the room of people to see.

"The Higher Powers have guided them, and this one," I gently shook the newest arrival, "was painted with the paint from the smoke people. I have and will hold them, almighty, in my hands. Let us pray."

Heads bowed as I spoke a prayer. "Light of light. Moonbeam of night. Shelter of souls, I come to you now. Bring my body, my soul, and bounty, whole. Guide and unravel with his grace, the shields of protection, to Amethyst in sight. Bring shelter to the twin unbound and find grace within to protect the darkness around. Amen."

"Amen," came from the group.

"Amethyst. Do you accept this charm?" I held up the necklace I had given to Jade at the kiosk.

"Yes, Grandmamma. I do." She lifted her hair so I could clasp it around her neck securely. Her gaze met Kades. "Don't worry, Kade. I know." Kade responded by wagging his tail.

I wanted to ask more, but well, we were in the middle of a ceremony. It could wait.

"I, Marissa, Oracle of the Higher Powers, also accept this charm." I put my hair up already, so clasping the chain was easy, even with my old hands. The necklaces were to be worn tonight.

Taking one of Amethyst's hands in one of mine and placing my other hand on top of Kade's head, I began. "What's done is done, can now be undone. A guard and children once one unravels now to lift the spell. Although joined become separated and unbound within this circle now, Higher Powers reveal. Let your life be your own. Whatever powers bound, let unfold. Your body is free. Your mind is yours. I unbind you, Amethyst, now and forever. I give you a part of me that has always been yours." I could feel heat invade the circle and watched the lights shine brightly around us.

Amethyst's eyes grew enormous. And she tried to deny part of what I had just done. What the others could not feel, but she could. She knew...

A quick flash of light, and suddenly we all stood in a dark room.

"Grant and Tristan, go turn on the lights; they'll work."

Tristan stood next to the light switch, which he had turned on. "Where's Kade?"

"He had to go," Amy mumbled.

"Is it done?" Nonny asked.

"Yes, it's done." I hugged Amy; she didn't know whether to cry or smile.

"You'll be fine," I whispered to her. "You had to know."

I felt her nod. "I love you, Grandmamma." A few tears dripped down my cheek. Kade was gone, and Amy had to deal with everything going on inside her.

"Jade will not be happy," Tristan muttered.

"She'll see him again. You tell her that." Amy, still hugging me, told Tristan. Nonny and Grant came closer, and Amy went to accept each of their hugs.

"How do you feel?" Grant asked his daughter.

"Different." Amy looked back at me. How do you express how it feels to be part of the grace of God? You just can't. I smiled at her in understanding and placed my finger over my lips. Grant and Nonny probably weren't ready to deal with that part of their daughter quiet yet. We all have a place in His plan, but sometimes there were better times to explain that.

"Is it okay if I go outside?" Amy asked quietly when the embracing had ended.

"That sounds wonderful. Fresh air," Nonny exclaimed before remembering her audience didn't need fresh air. Even Amy's requirement might have been questionable after the ritual.

Amy gently placed her hand on her mother's arm. "Actually, can you give me some time alone? Just a little, and then I'll come back in for you. We can go for a walk as we used to in Idaho."

Nonny seemed a little surprised at her daughter's request. "Sure, Amy. I'll wait in the front room with Jade. I should check on her, anyway." Nonny pushed past us and left the room.

"I don't know if it's safe for you to be alone. Mom?" Grant sounded like he hoped I would say no.

"She'll be fine." So, I told Grant and then told Amy, "Don't worry your parents too long."

She smiled and nodded before leaving the room without another word.

"She's safe here," I reassured Grant. He was still looking at the door where Amy had left.

"She's all grown up now. So fast." Grant crossed his arms in front of him and turned toward me. "There's something different about her. It's more than the fact that her powers, or whatever they may be, have been unbound." Did Grant know? He stared me down, but I wasn't about to budge.

"Excuse me, Jade is calling for me." Tristan tapped his finger on his head. Their telepathy was in use, as it was a soulmate thing.

"Yeah, yeah, rub it in as usual," Grant replied as Tristan left. Finally, it was Grant, and I left in the room, so I shut the door.

"You think that door is going to keep the vampires from hearing what you have to say?" Grant asked lightly.

"They're busy. I think I'm safe," I told Grant as I headed for the pouches on the desk.

"So, you were with the smoke people for almost ten days?" Grant strode to my side, looking at the pouches where I had placed my hands.

“Not the entire time. Probably very little of that time,” I confessed.

“But the pouches they came from them? The Chief?” Grant wondered.

“Yes and no; from… him. But there was a smoke woman who spoke as we do. She was the one who gave the pouches to me. I already had to use part of one during the quest placed on me. I don’t think they planned that. They are now out of this until….” Life or death was upon us.

“Until?” Grant repeated.

“Until I don’t know for sure.” Scooping up the pouches, I headed for the couch. I was beyond exhausted and drained of the last drop of magic within me.

“So, what happened? How do you know they didn’t plan whatever happened during your quest?” Grant pushed.

“I don’t know. But I had three roads to choose from; I chose Amethyst’s and….” Should I tell him about his siblings’ full graves and the empty grave for his daughter? And then it hit me!

“Oh!” Raising my hands, which were still holding the pouches to my lips, I couldn’t believe what I had missed.

“What?” Grant came over and sat beside me. “Did you have a vision?”

“No.” I could barely get the words out. Then, lowering my hands, I explained, “I just remembered something.”

“Like?” Grant wanted to know. Should I?

“There wasn’t a grave for Jet.” He wouldn’t understand, anyway.

His eyebrows came together in question, and he sat back on the couch. “And that makes sense to me how? I mean, I’m glad there isn’t a grave anywhere for Jet. Can you go back just a little here?”

“I was sent on a quest, but I was told I would know when to use these things.” I held the pouches up. “At a later date, I assumed. I’m almost positive.” I scrunched my face up. “Oh hell, what do I know?”

“Anyway… moving on.” Grant waved his hands to tell me to get on with the story.

"Okay, so like I said, I came to this pivotal point in the quest. Left was Jet, forward was Micah, and to the right was Amethyst. Well, the smoke people had mentioned Amethyst, so I figured that was a hint for me to go that way. So, I walked and…." Then, there… was a knock on the door.

"Mary? Nonny wants to know if Amy should still be outside." Mandy asked.

"She's fine. I would tell Nonny that if she is that concerned, to go on out. We'll be out shortly."

"Okay." I heard Mandy walking away from the door and back down the hall.

"Where was I?" I asked Grant.

"The smoke people hinted for you to take Amethyst's way." He was deep into the story, wanting more.

"Right. Oh! And I forgot to tell you they brought me back to the age I was when I met Diamonté." Grant nodded and motioned for me to continue.

"So, I came to my old town, the town with mud houses and everything. I mean, it was ancient, and yet everything was simply perfect. Like people still were living there." I took a breath; I felt I was talking like a speedboat.

"I decided this had to be about my first meeting with Diamonté, so I went to my old house. Nothing. So I went to the place where we first met." This time, I paused because I plain hated this part.

"I crossed the little river and came to the clearing and…." I couldn't say it.

"And you saw something." Grant thought for a second. "Graves."

I nodded.

"But how did you know what you were looking at? Jet's grave wasn't there, you said?" Grant wasn't putting the dots together. He was forcing me to have to connect with them.

"I saw the graves of your siblings, Grant. All marked graves. And even those for the children I didn't even remember until I stood right in front of them." I could feel my eyes brimming with tears. Grant got up and found some tissues on the desk.

“And then…” I looked into Grant’s eyes. “I saw the empty open grave with a headstone for our precious Amy.”

Grant paced, flustered. “I’m going to kill that son of a bitch.” Grant’s fists were held tight to his side.

“Sit, Grant. There’s more.” I patted the seat next to me. It wouldn’t do any good for him not to keep his head straight. There would be a time to reap. For his father, I was sure. But he needed to think straight and be rational for now. I shivered; I couldn’t help it.

“What?” he asked, sitting next to me but far from relaxed.

I returned to tell the story. He would hear soon enough. “The realization I had ago was like I said, Jet didn’t have a grave.”

“But there was a grave for everyone else?” Grant asked again for details, to be sure.

“Yes. Just not one for Jet. And then, I went back to my house because I didn’t know what to do. So, I laid on my old bed and ended up lying on these. I dumped the pouch out and showed him the amethyst gems.”

“Okay?” Grant looked confused.

“I know. I still don’t know what to make of the gems. But there’s more. Keegan and some other ‘things’ or whatever you want to call them rode in on horses.”

“Did they see you?” Grant looked mortified.

“No. But, they smelled a human. So, before they could figure anything out, I drank a little of this.” I handed the red-filled vial to him.

“Blood?” Now he looked confused.

“It stopped my heart, Grant. They couldn’t smell me, and then they moved on. It’s what saved me, but also what dropped me back here with you. But the pain coming out of it as my heart started beating again.” I shook my head. “I can’t explain it. But I wasn’t supposed to use it until we got where Diamonté is.”

“With Keegan, who is with Jet, who is with Micah, where all the Drobny things are.” He closed his eyes and dropped his head forward.

“Shit,” he muttered.

"So, you're supposed to drink it, so Diamonté doesn't know you're there? Is it you or a human thing?"

It was a good question, and I wasn't sure the answer. "Either or?" I shrugged.

"So, let me get this straight. My son is my father's prodigy?" Grant stood up, unable to control his nerves.

"And my daughter? Who is she?" Grant demanded, his voice getting loud.

I shrugged, hoping he wouldn't see my lie. You bet your stars I knew who Amethyst was.

"I have to go!" He stormed out of the room.

I sure hoped Jade was ready for travel. Unfortunately, we had no time to waste.

Chapter Fourteen

Mary

While shaking her gently, Tristan sternly said, "Jade, you need to feed. I won't take no as an answer anymore." Tristan's face became masked with concern. Jade pulled away from his hand. She hadn't left the couch all day while we had talked of plans to take down the palace and the evil inside. Of course, while saving Jet and Micah. Our options were limited due to time and those we could trust, only ourselves. The Shadow Night had been laced with a blanket of poison by Diamonté.

"No, Tristan. I'm sick of being sick. I'll just puke it up." Her voice was raspy from doing just that for four days straight.

Though I was about as useless as Jade now, I still knew many more than either of them regarding vampire pregnancy. Walking over to Jade, I placed my hand on her forehead. I used to be able to feel the tyro within when I lived at the palace. I couldn't feel the little one, but I wasn't surprised.

"Tristan is right, Jade. Even a very minimal offering, no matter how long you can hold it down, will still make it to your child." I was muttering, as a mother would to her child. I wanted Jade and the tyro to be healthy.

Jade didn't move for a moment. "Fine," she muttered, although she didn't roll over.

"I don't want to bring a carcass in here." Tristan looked uncomfortable.

"I don't understand why we can't use the bagged product?" Nonny asked everyone.

"She needs fresh during this time. That's all. It will stay down longer despite what Jade believes." Tristan told Nonny.

"It still comes back up." So Jade reminded all of us.

Running a hand through his hair, Tristan thought about what to do. "I guess I can muster something up without bringing the carcass in here. Mandy, can you bring me a big pan and a glass or something?"

"Sure." Mandy scrambled, not wanting to see too much of what was to come, I was sure. She returned from the kitchen with a big pot and a coffee mug.

"Will this work?" she asked as she handed them to Tristan.

"Yes." He left through the front door with the items.

"I'll go help," Grant said, leaving us women in the room, except for Amy. She had been out on another one of her walks.

Amy entered the house and looked around. Our gazes met, and I could tell she wanted to talk. I shook my head and looked at Jade. Thankfully, Amy understood and took the chair that had been placed next to Jade at her head.

"Hey, Jade," Amy said, stroking her aunt's cheek. She paused at her forehead the way I had shortly before. Her eyes grew wide. I put my fingers to my lips, telling her to keep quiet about what she was experiencing. Nonny watched her daughter and best friend with great interest.

"What?" Nonny asked Amy.

"Nothing. I mean," Amy didn't know what to say after I'd told her to be quiet.

"Mean what? You can tell me." Nonny urged her.

"Yeah," Jade croaked. "I'm not dead here, and even I feel something." She grabbed Amy's hand before Amy could pull it away. Jade had little strength, but she held Amy's hand to her forehead. "Tell me."

Amy looked at me for help. Shrugging, I told them, "Whatever you hear between us women, you keep it bound in private here. Do not tell the guys. Okay? Jade, somehow you have to hold Tristan back." We found with Jade and Tristan that her pregnancy allowed him access to her he hadn't had before. Their soulmate link became powerful.

Jade rolled over, still holding Amy's hand to her head. "I'll try."

"That's all we can ask for; there's a lot at stake coming up with Micah. That is where his focus needs to be." I nodded once more to Jade, and she agreed with a nod back. A fresh look of pain came over her face at the reminder of Micah.

I gave Amy the go-ahead. "Well, umm…" Amy closed her eyes for a moment and then opened them to speak. "He's strong now, but won't be if you don't take care of him, Jade. He's hungry. But, umm…" Amy removed her hand. "Wow, he's brilliant." She smiled and looked my way. "That is so amazing." I nodded.

"He? It's a boy?" Jade was pleased. Nonny was smiling but kept quiet, perhaps out of shock at what her daughter was doing. "What was it that surprised you?"

"Just feelings… it's like…." Amy began to tell her, but the guys came through the door. They were a little bloody, but carrying the pot and coffee mug.

"Okay, momma," Tristan stated as he handed the mug to Jade. "Drink up." Surprising Tristan, she smiled and took the mug, and downed it all in one slug. "More," she said, handing the mug back to him.

"I'm out of here," Mandy said. "I think I'll go home for a bit. Clean up, get some rest. I'll be back in the morning." Mandy didn't care for the sight of blood. Go figure.

Watching Amy perform just now had confirmed everything I already knew. "Amy?" She looked up. I motioned with my head for her to follow me from the room. No one was paying any attention to either of us any longer. So that made what I was going to give her that much easier.

Once the two of us were back in my multi-use room, I spoke to her freely as I shut and locked the door. "Like that would do much good." She kidded me.

"Well, it makes me feel better," I told her quietly.

Making my way to where the amethyst gems still lay on a table, I gathered them up and put them into one pouch from the smoke people. Amy had followed me over and watched intently.

"Is this about what happened with Jade and me just now?" She asked me quietly.

"Yes." I put the last of the gems into the pouch and handed them to her.

"These are yours," I stated matter-of-factly to her.

She hesitated a moment before taking them. "I'm not sure what you want me to do with them."

"So many different and amazing beings have graced you. What defines you inside is something that I cannot even understand. But I can help guide you," I whispered.

"I thought it was the powers you unbound like Jet." She looked at me, confused.

Shaking my head, I told her, "There's more. Much more. What you have goes beyond what even Jade or your brother Jet hold." Her eyes widened.

"Jade, Micah, and all her future tyros are pureblood Royals. They define the Shadow Night. That is the way it has been and will always be. Well, until the Higher Powers decide otherwise or…." Shuddering, I let myself think of the place we would travel to handle Diamonté and the dark that followed him.

"You, Amethyst, are a part of that, but you're also a part of me. The calling you feel is that of my calling as an Oracle Goddess. A part of a much bigger plan than Diamonté knew. Don't think for a second; our paths are not already created before time. It's merely our destiny that awaits. The web that has been created is so much bigger than any of us can understand." Amy continued to stare at me, wide-eyed.

"Good always knows more than evil. Just keep that in mind, whether you believe what I'm telling you. However, just because we know more, it doesn't always protect us the way it should. What we will walk into where your brother Jet is, is a place of death." I took her hands in mine, with hers still clutching the amethyst gems inside the pouch.

"I'm scared," she confided.

"Me, too. And we should be. It is one hell of a time to confront all this with what little we know. But I guarantee you. The Higher Powers do not want to screw up this ecosystem with our extinction. Only God can play God. We are in a war, Amethyst, where loss is always a possibility."

"And these?" She shook the gems.

"You'll need them someday after I'm gone." Then, pulling her to me, we hugged tightly.

"One other thing, Amy." She pulled back to look me in the eye. "Keep this all on the down-low for now. The less anyone knows, the safer you'll be."

"Okay," she agreed.

I had the essence stone still. Taking it from the table as well, I tried to hand it to her.

She shook her head. "I hear a voice inside my head telling me it is not mine to take."

Now it was my turn to look confused. "That makes little sense."

"I don't know what to tell you, Grandmamma." She walked over and ran her hands over the front of the spell book. "Can I borrow this?"

"Take it. It's yours." Amy scooped the book up along with her pouch. "I'll keep it hidden, don't worry."

"You'd better. It's the last of its kind."

"I know. They told me." And with that comment, she left the room. I was left scratching my head. Who told her what? The smoke people? Who?

This was all the warning I wanted to give her without scaring her out of her mind. Diamonté would be after my granddaughter, foremost. Keegan, he was another story. Next, I had to monitor my Jade. I might be powerless and nothing more than a dying human now, but I hadn't lost my memory.

* * *

Most of us were around the kitchen table, talking and digesting plans. "I still haven't figured out how everything leads us back to Idaho," Nonny said.

"Are you kidding? That's easy. It's where Jade was for eighteen years." Grant answered her in a way to make her feel stupid.

Out of nowhere, and not even quick enough for Grant to stop, Nonny slapped Grant's face. He grabbed her hand, though, before she could retreat. The silence in the room was deafening.

We all were looking from one to the other, waiting for one of them to say something. But then, I saw in Nonny something I hadn't seen since I first met her. Life!

Nonny tried to take her hand back. Grant rubbed it with his thumb, not letting go but softening his hold.

"Feel better?" he finally asked her.

"Not too much. I know it didn't hurt you. But it was a little satisfying." Nonny's voice quivered. She was close to tears, but she kept control, thrusting her chin up.

"Is there anyone else you would like to hit? Or is it just me?" Grant asked Nonny.

"Just you. However, I blame the whole Shadow Night for their stupidity and how they treated me, Mary, and Mandy. I hold you personally responsible for where Jet and Micah are." Nonny pulled her hand back abruptly, and Grant let go.

The ambiance in the room portrayed pain and betrayal.

"You left them out of this." Grant motioned to Tristan and Jade.

"We don't have time for your drama, Nonny." Tristan was pissed. "How dare you bring this all up now? All I want is my daughter back. We'll deal with everything else once this is over." Tristan stood and flung the chair aside.

Grant exploded. "How dare you do this to all of us now? Your issues should've been privately discussed with me. You have no right to talk like that to them or any of us! What's done is done! You should be happy! You were lucky not to be under their, whatever it was. Being out of there and here with you, I see that now! Knock the shit off! You're my wife, like it or not, and we'll deal with all this later when we have all our family back and the asshole from hell gone!"

"Grant. That's enough." I put myself out in Nonny's defense. We had done much more arguing than planning. It was wearing on the group morale.

Jade dry-heaved in the other room. Nonny excused herself quietly, thankful to leave the fighting. She was probably regretting it as well.

"Grant. She's human. Like me, now. Not dumb." I commented quietly.

Grant ran a hand through his already messed-up hair. "It's agitating, having to answer dumb questions, and then her hitting me and going nuts like that." Finally, he stopped and placed a napkin on the table. "I always hoped the blood mixing from our children would make her a little more like me."

His admission with his daughter sitting right there was probably like a slap to her face. I looked at her. The rest of us left in the room looked at her.

"It's fine. I get it." She tried to wave it off. Grant realized what he had said a little too late.

"I didn't mean it to be derogatory to you." Instead, he reached out to her.

"It's fine, Dad. I wouldn't want to be made any differently. How you feel is how you feel."

"But that's not how I meant it." Grant continued to explain.

Tristan came back into the room, picking his chair back up and sitting down. His temper had cooled.

"It's fine, Dad. Let's move on with the plans so we can move on. What you have all been discussing still has a zero benefit." Amy sounded old and wise, and to my surprise, they all listened to her. Was she using magic? I couldn't be sure. I didn't know what she could do or was capable of, as I was sure she was unclear as well. But whatever she had stumbled across seemed to work fine.

I tried to catch her eye, but she wouldn't look at me.

"It doesn't matter what our genetic make-up is. These years have not been kind to any of us. We have all lived a lie. We have my brother, a true Royal cousin, and some old death to handle. We are going to lose the whole surprise effect if we don't get a move on because the Sawtooth Mountains are not sitting in the yard outside." Amy folded her arms in front of her chest.

"Tristan, you're the King of the Shadow Night. Dad, you're in charge of the strength that protects them. So I don't understand why suddenly you two can't figure out a plan that works with everything you guys have done." Everyone nodded, and Grant and Tristan looked at each other.

"She's right," Grant admitted to Tristan.

"How did we do it before?" Tristan asked Grant.

"I don't know. We just did it. Our plan changed so many times from what we were expecting." Grant still played with the napkin. I grasped his hand in mine.

"Stop it!" The room went quiet. Nonny appeared with Jade in the doorway.

"I'm ready to go," Jade told them. "We have to get going." Tristan stood up and went to his pregnant wife.

"Listen to Amy. She's right. You all are playing hardball in here. You're overthinking everything because it is our children. But if we don't get going and figure it out, there won't be anything left to recognize. Micah is in the hands of the damnation devil himself. Who knows what they are doing to her? Jet, they have been working him over since the day they met him."

"Perhaps things are not as bad as we feel they may be for them right now?" Nonny sounded hopeful.

"And perhaps they're worse." Tristan shook his head, as if not wanting to hear his voice say the words.

"They'll know we are coming," Amy said.

"But they won't know when." Mandy piped in.

"It doesn't matter. They have nothing to lose and everything to gain. What I don't understand is what key or keys they're missing. Jade? Tristan?" Grant stood up and paced.

Amy looked over, catching my eye. I shook my head ever so slightly, telling her to keep her mouth shut. I hoped no one saw.

"Well, let's get that massive passenger van all loaded and get the heck out of Dodge," Amy said with excitement.

"Yes." Jade croaked. "Let's go!"

The spirit was there. Finally, just taking the leap to do it and figuring it out on the way seemed to make everyone happy, except for one.

"Well, I'll root for you." Mandy couldn't go. She would be dead in a heartbeat.

"I have some things to gather up. Mandy, why don't you come to help me." It would most likely be our last goodbye.

"It won't take us long, Mary. Are ten minutes enough for you?" Tristan asked as he helped Jade to a chair. "We need to get the food supply we have here on ice and a few personal items."

"Ten minutes?" There was no way I could be ready in ten minutes. I had personal items to take care of, as well as talking with Mandy.

"That's not fair." Mandy protested. "I have spent forever with this woman, and you're going to whisk her away too fast." Mandy was crying.

"You'll see her again." Grant came to Tristan's side.

"I won't, and you know it." Mandy gulped back tears.

I looked back at them as I took her arm to leave the kitchen. "I'll be out soon enough. But it won't be ten minutes."

"We are wasting time, Mary." Tristan pushed.

"You had plenty of time to waste, sitting here arguing. Don't lose your damn humanity over a few minutes!" I would not listen to their crap. I pulled Mandy along after me. They would get over it as soon as we were five miles out of town.

* * *

Mandy had sat on my bed watching me pack a small bag.

"Mandy, I'm going to leave most of my Oracle items here."

"So, you think you'll be back, then?" Mandy sounded hopeful through the tears.

"I would hate to have you write me off so soon." I didn't want to leave a false hope that I would be back. But maybe I would be okay. Being human, though, didn't give me warm fuzzies about going into battle with the bastards of hell. Diamonté would have to be taken out. He was done hurting our family.

"Can you hold fast to a secret either way?" I asked as I placed the essence crystal into a smaller jewelry pouch. I had thought about keeping it on me, but it seemed to clash with the feelings of the necklace I still wore from the ritual.

I sat next to Mandy on the bed, with my hand grasping the necklace. It was a sign; I was sure of it. Removing it from my neck, I placed it into Mandy's hand.

"Mary, no. That is your protection." She tried to force it back into my hand.

"I don't need it, Mandy. Wear it and keep it safe, along with what I'm going to tell you."

Mandy stared at me, waiting. "What, Mary?"

"Amy will be back. I hope. And she will need everything of mine." Mandy opened her mouth, and I knew she would want to argue about my return.

"Whether or not I'm back, she will return for all of this. You won't be alone, I promise. She is so much more than I ever could be in a world like today. I can't see the future, but I want you to find your happiness. The family will find and surround you wherever you are."

Mandy reached out and clung to me. "Godspeed, Mary. I love you."

"I love you too, Mandy. Thank you so much for everything." I cried with her, finally. "This isn't goodbye. See you soon."

Pulling back, I stood up at the loud knocking at my bedroom door. "Let's go, Mary." Tristan opened the door, not waiting.

"Take my bag, please, Tristan." I zipped the bag up I had packed.

"Come on." I held my hand out for Mandy to take and walk out with me.

"I can't," Mandy said, not leaving the bed.

"You can, and you will. Now come tell us goodbye and wish us Godspeed." I pulled her up, and we went outside. Everyone was loaded except me and, "Where's Nonny?"

Grant was in the driver's seat and didn't turn his head. "Probably inside the house or around back. I don't know. She isn't coming."

"It's just as well. She's human." Tristan said dryly.

"Should I go back in and talk to her? Shouldn't she go with us? Jet is her son, for crying out loud. I can't believe this." I climbed back out.

"Stay, Mom. We have to go. We need to go. And I don't have time for this crap. We have kids that need us and stuff."

"I've got this, Mary." Mandy hugged me one more time. "See you soon."

I wanted Nonny in this car, but I was in no shape to take on a group of pissed-off vampires. So, nodding back, I said, "Love you, Mandy."

"Bye, y'all!" Mandy tried to sound chipper but seemed anxious now to find Nonny.

"Bye. Take care." Grant and Tristan told her.

I was catching Mandy's eyes one last time to see her one last time. She had been my lifeline. Breathing deeply, I held back the tears.

Mandy shut the door, and we were on our way!

Chapter Fifteen

Nonny

I did it. I hit my husband and cursed the people I loved for most of my life sending them all off to handle business. Their business… my kids. I wanted to throw up because I abandoned everyone who mattered to me and left my best friend to cope with the child giving her havoc in the womb. I wouldn't even witness the birth.

I ran and ran until I couldn't run any further. Then, collapsing onto the cold, hard ground, I let my body retch in pain. I didn't deserve to live. I was a complete failure in all ways humanly possible.

I lay in the dirt, not even moving out of my vomit for a long time. Finally, it was Mandy, with her flashlight bouncing around, that pulled me to full awareness.

"Nonny?" Mandy kept calling for me. Finally, after a few more calls, I allowed myself to answer her. I didn't want her freezing her butt off all night looking for me.

"Here," I answered her, not too loudly. "Mandy, I'm over here." So I talked until the spotlight found me.

“Good Lord, Nonny!” Mandy came and stood over me. “You look like hell.”

“I feel like it too,” I admitted.

“Come on. Let me help you up.” Mandy tried to grab me.

“Leave me here. I don’t deserve to live.”

“Stop it, Nonny. You’re a wife and a mother, and I have had enough of this shit to last a lifetime. I lost the only woman who ever meant anything to me tonight. Now, I mean it. I don’t want any shit right now. So stand up and shut up. I love you, Nonny, just come back to the house. We’ll get you cleaned up and a cocktail in your hand. I need you.”

As she spoke to me, I obeyed her orders and did as she asked. Then, we walked together for a while.

“I can’t believe how far out you came.” Her teeth were chattering. “Shit, I can’t believe I even found you.”

Mandy continued to talk until we came to the back porch of Mary’s house. I had never heard her swear so much!

“Let’s go in here. I would rather be here tonight than at my place. Okay?”

I nodded, still quiet. My things were here, anyway.

“Let’s use the bathroom in Mary’s room. I’m going to run you a bath. Come on.” Mandy took my hand and led me to Mary’s room.

“Can you undress and get in if I get the bath going?” Mandy’s look softened. “You’re going to be okay. In no time, this will all be over with, and everyone will be back together.”

I looked at Mandy. Did she believe that?

“Can you get in by yourself? You’re quiet.” She asked me again.

“I can. Yes.” I whispered.

She nodded and went to the bathroom to start the water running in the tub. “Mary has some nice-smelling bath salts to calm you down, and I have everything here that you should need. Just put this robe on when you’re ready to come out.”

Mandy came out of the bathroom, smiling slightly. "I know you feel hopeless… worthless… whatever. But I'm glad you're here. And you're none of the above. Okay, don't lock the door, just in case. I'll have a cocktail for us to relax and talk with when you're ready." She waited for me to acknowledge her, so I nodded an okay.

Mandy stood at the door, then softly closed it, and walked down the hall, leaving me to my thoughts and a hot bath.

Undressing by the tub, I let the water keep filling. The bath salts smelled amazing and bubbled up high on the top lip of the tub. The steam was hot and fogging up the mirror, and I was grateful not to have to look myself in the eye right now.

Climbing in and shutting the water off, I melted away into the water, immersing myself entirely below the water. I stayed under for as long as my breath would allow.

Mary had a bath pillow attached to the back of her tub. Surfacing, I laid against it and closed my eyes. Feeling defeated, lost, hollow, I had no more tears to shed. How had I gotten here? To this awful place in my life?

Even my thoughts drifted back and forth. One minute I was young, with a best friend named Jade, living in Lewiston. The next, I was a mother of two, sharing a life with the man of my dreams.

I guess I fell asleep for a spell because suddenly Mandy appeared in the bathroom doorway, calling for me, and the bathwater had turned quite cold.

"Sorry. I knocked, but you didn't answer, and I was concerned." Mandy tried not to look at me as she spoke.

"It's okay. I must have been in here for a long time. Guess I fell asleep." I yawned, surprised at how under the weather I felt after napping.

"Not too long. Ten minutes, maybe?" She tried to figure it out. "I have the cocktails ready, though. Are you ready to come to sit with me and talk?"

"Ten minutes? Maybe? Hmm." The water felt like ice. "Are you sure? Feel this water. It was boiling when I got in. I need to get out. I wrapped the towel around me as I climbed out.

Mandy came over and dipped her hand in, and said, "Wow! I don't know how you were even sitting in here. My butt would've been out way before it got this cold." Mandy wiped her hands on a hand towel at the sink.

"Weird. I guess it's up to the cocktails to warm us up. Meet you in the kitchen." Mandy brushed off the puzzle of the water temperature and left.

It was weird. But maybe I had been in longer than Mandy thought. I put lotion on quickly and wrapped myself in Mary's soft pink robe. A cocktail sounded good right now, and so did a friend.

* * *

We were two glasses into our therapy of cocktails and talking. I could feel the heated flush from the alcohol on my cheeks. There hadn't been a lot of talking, just drinking. I couldn't speak for Mandy, but I didn't know where to begin. We sat sipping on the couch.

"Are you going to go back to being an accountant, then?" Of course, that was wholly off-topic, but I broke the silence to let her know I was ready to talk or cry.

Mandy shrugged. "I never stopped altogether. A lot of what I do now is more consulting. I can continue to do that like I have been, working from home, here and there. It's not like we needed the money or anything." She let the last sentence hang. One perk of being related to vampires is you have funds as needed.

"I'm sure Mary kept you plenty busy. Especially lately, with her health deteriorating so quickly now." Way to go, Nonny. Nothing like a reminder in the short time Mary has been gone that she probably won't see her again.

Mandy gingerly wiped under her eyes so the tear wouldn't escape. "Yeah. It has been quite different this go around."

"Sorry, I wasn't thinking. I was trying to keep my thoughts away from my family." My children's lives, and a husband who doesn't think much of me right now, are all gone. Who even knew what my parents were up to these days, either. They had quit trying to push their way into the lives of their only daughter and grandchildren after that last incident. While their memories had been taken from them about that whole dramatic experience, everything else had changed, too. I had told myself it was for the best. Now, I wondered about all that, too. I should've fought for my family then, and I should've fought for my family now. I guess I couldn't learn anything.

"Why didn't you go, Nonny?" Mandy collected herself.

I took a long drink from my wineglass, emptying it, and then reaching for the bottle to fill it again. There were a lot of reasons I'd pulled out at the last minute. But the biggest one was because I wasn't ready to face the demented demons that had made me turn into a coward.

"I don't think I can mentally or physically compete with what they are facing. What if I caused the death of someone there because I'm human?" While that was all true, it didn't exactly say "coward," in bright letters to Mandy.

Mandy nodded in agreement as I spoke and then added, "True. But wouldn't you at least have liked to have been closer? I mean, your parents' house is in the same state they are going to."

"I hadn't thought of that, in all honesty. I was thinking selfishly, I guess." This girl talk was coming out as cover-ups and little white lies. It was wrong, and I hadn't planned it. I had planned to come out and put it all out there. I was a coward!

"Well, it's something to think about, I guess. I love having you here. We are family through Mary, but it all feels wrong to me." Mandy cupped her wineglass in her hand, peering into the liquid-like the answers were floating on top.

"Does it? I mean, if you think I should go, I can." Did she want me to go? Had she been lying to me as well and didn't want me here?

"Oh, no! That's not what I meant, Nonny. Everything is coming out wrong." Mandy sounded frustrated.

"I know what you mean," I stated the obvious. "I feel guilty, Mandy." My eyes welled with tears. "I kicked my parents from my life, my husband, and my children. I don't understand how all this could've happened." Staying strong so the tears wouldn't come was hard, but I didn't feel I deserved to cry.

"What do you mean? I mean, I know you're upset at how you handled things here, but your parents, too?" Mandy looked horrified.

"Yes." I nodded. "Back when we lived at the palace, when the kids were getting older. Jet, the birthday party, and the Drobny clan. Even Jade and Tristan. It was a horrible mess, and I know it wasn't Jade's fault, but I had to blame someone. It was horrible, and my parents got tied up, literally, at our house, and Amy and I ran out of there." I took a breath before continuing to pour the scene out, and even I couldn't believe it as I said everything. "They took my parents' memory away, and I think, even more than that. I don't know what they all did." Covering my face, I spoke through my hands. "My parents don't even act like they want to see us. I think something is wrong with them. I'm a coward, Mandy! A doormat! I let everyone control me, and I didn't fight!" The tears came. I had admitted defeat. "I hurt everyone who comes around me. Maybe it's me and not anyone else!"

Mandy's arm came around me. "Don't say that, Nonny. Don't talk like that. It's all nonsense. Quit crying and sit up. Do you want to quit calling yourself a coward? Then do it right now." There was no tenderness in Mandy's voice. She was cradling me, but she demanded that I listen.

Mandy sat me back against the couch as I hiccupped once. Finally, I found my quiet place and shut up.

"Now, you hear me out. This life is our life. It's short for us humankind, but it doesn't mean it demands any less respect. Nonny, you're the exception to the house rules, just like Mary. That is something to be proud of and admire within yourself. You're special, and so are your children. Your parents gave you life, but your path was already waiting. So, enough of the 'if I had done this or that..' This is life, and it's our lives here on this couch. What's done is done. We may not have much to do but sit around here and wait for our loved ones to return. But, we chose this. You chose this! It will not change, and whatever happens, and it will happen, just like I know Mary won't be back. God help me. I know she won't. But, sitting here with you and listening made me realize that our destiny is right here and right now."

Mandy took a breather. I was trying to take in everything as quickly as she was spitting it out. "We are different."

"We are different." Mandy agreed. "I don't know if they're going to be saving the world or just the people we hold near and dear. Nonny, I do not know what anyone's plans are, and whose lives are at stake, and whose lives are being altered by dark forces."

"Do you think there are more than my children's lives at stake? Besides Grant's and Mary's? I mean, of those who matter to us personally." I had to wonder if Mandy knew what she was talking about that I didn't know about.

"All I know is Diamonté doesn't want to stop until… who knows what will make him stop? So I think it has a lot more to do with everyone other than Jade. It's a whole combination at play that I don't think even Mary knew about as the Oracle."

"But, Amy." What was my sweet Amy's role in all this? They had Jet. They had Micah. Were they taking Amy into a trap?

"Jet, Amy, Micah, I think this new generation has something bigger in the plan for them." Mandy must have been on the same brain wavelength as me. "Why did it take them leaving for us to think like this?"

Mandy shrugged. "It could be they still have some kind of hex thing or whatever you all have been calling it on them."

"Not Amy. I don't think she ever had it." But in my heart, I knew she was safe.

Silently, I sent a prayer out to her, hoping she heard my plea to be safe, come back, and stay with me.

"Maybe I should've gone, at least to Idaho, and stayed with my parents. Make things right if I could and be closer if anything happened to any of them." Thinking about it, I said, "We both could've gone there."

Mandy shook her head. "My home is here. Whatever happens with Mary, I need to be here."

I wondered why she thought that if Mary died, something unexpected would be here. Who knew? "Hmm. Well, I should probably stay here since this is where they know I'm. If anyone still cares." I frowned at my remark.

"They care, Nonny. It's a hex, or spell, or just plain evil that is causing all this. What happened to that positive woman I used to know?" Mandy smiled a little.

"She got beat down and turned around." I couldn't tell her where my old self had gone. "Maybe they got to me too."

"No, I don't think so. You need to think positive," Mandy said.

Shrugging it off, I had an idea. “I could fly. They can’t fly, but I can.”

“You don’t know where they are going, though, or where they will be.” Mandy wasn’t sure where to go with this idea.

“I mean, I could go home and see my parents and see what is wrong. I feel so much clearer suddenly. Everything is becoming clearer. I think you were right. Something is tied to them and left when they left here.” Or maybe I was thinking wishfully.

“I don’t know.” Did she think I shouldn’t go anywhere now? She was the one who’d brought it up in the first place, after all.

“You said I should go.” I reminded her.

“Well, after our conversation, I’m rethinking that. I kind of was talking earlier. I didn’t think you would, and I didn’t know any of the circumstances you filled me in on.”

“It might be a good thing to go do, though. Maybe I could help after being such a dummy.” I felt hopeful.

“Maybe you would make things worse. If your parents have something wrong, you wouldn’t be safe, Nonny. So forget about it.” Mandy had utterly changed her thinking. “Do not go.”

“I don’t know. It’s something to think about. We’re talking about my flesh and blood. Maybe they’re stopping there first before hitting the Idaho Sawtooth Mountains. I would be fine. The danger isn’t here or with my parents. It’s where the children are being kept, probably not against their will. Damn Diamonté!”

“Forget it, Nonny. Let’s think of something else.” Mandy looked frightened now. I would change the subject, but only to please her. When she went to bed, I would see about airfare to Idaho. I wouldn’t be putting Mandy in danger. I would help my entire family out. They would see that.

“Okay, I give up for now. Let’s make something to eat. I’m starving.” Mandy looked at me for a moment and smiled. She had bought it.

“Okay. I feel better now, don’t you?” She stood and stretched.

“Yep. Completely.” Standing up, I followed her into the kitchen.

* * *

The seeds had been planted in my head, and all I needed now was a plan and a plane. The rest I would figure out as I went.

Mandy surprised me by not staying the night at Mary's house.

"I can't be here tonight. Maybe tomorrow night?" She stood in the doorway's frame. The chilly wind breezed in between the cracks. I shivered, as I wasn't bundled up as she was.

"It's fine, Mandy. I would prefer my own space, anyway. It's been a shitty day, and I feel like I want to be left alone with my thoughts." I did a long fake yawn and stretched. "Go on before you freeze me out of here after I just got all warmed up."

"Okay." Mandy came back over for a last hug. "See ya in the morning, then." She waved, and I nodded and closed the door.

I went to Mary's office, where she had an old computer. I hoped it would work for finding me a plane ticket out of here. Sitting in front of the monitor, I hit the button to turn it on and waited for everything to load.

"Come on, you old dinosaur." The fear of being caught by Mandy still wasn't far from my mind. I didn't think she would come back right then, but my guilt kept me on point.

"Load already." The computer was taking forever. Or what seemed forever? Resting my hand on my chin, I closed my eyes to daydream about my plans for leaving here.

I would need a taxi to take me to Cincinnati Lunken Airport. It was a little over sixty miles, and I didn't want to leave a car in short-term parking since I didn't know when I would be back.

I rubbed my temples. I could feel a migraine coming on. "No headache. No migraine. Go away." I was trying to talk myself out of it. Like that would work.

"I'd better get some ibuprofen on board." I rechecked the computer and found it was still loading. Pushing the chair back, I headed to the kitchen for some medication and water to ease the pain now shooting through the right side of my head.

I pulled the bottle from the cabinet, dropping it on the floor. Then, cradling my hand against my head, I reached down for the medication.

"Stupid bottle." Muttering at the helpless bottle, I felt agitated now and downed a couple more than I should've, without filling a glass of water first.

My thoughts were all over the place: plane ticket, Idaho, vampires, my kids, my soulmate.

"What am I doing?" Standing over the kitchen sink, I looked out the darkened window. I couldn't see anything outside, but I heard the wind howl and felt loneliness.

"This sucks, Nonny. What are you going to do?" Go or stay. Now I wasn't sure. The darkness was scary. I wasn't sure I was tough enough to handle anything anymore. I was weak and human. Maybe it would be best if I let them all go. Let the pieces fall where they would. Perhaps this was my destiny to lose it all.

I heard sirens far away. Someone was getting help somewhere. There was a family out there getting the help they needed. Was it a child that was hurt? It made me wonder if I could live with myself if I stayed here, pretending that my life was normal.

I caught my reflection in the window. "Coward!" I stared at my reflection and didn't like what I saw. But I didn't want to be a coward. Running back to the office, I sat down in front of the computer that was done loading.

"Shit!" A password was needed. I hadn't thought about that. "Stupid dinosaur, you're not supposed to need a password to access you." Maybe it was a sign I shouldn't proceed any further. Stay here and be a… "You're not a coward. Figure it out, Nonny."

Placing my hands on the keyboard, I said to myself, "How about Amethyst?" But, no, that wasn't it.

"Grant." No.

"Shadow Night?" No.

"It's simple. I know it is. Those close to you should be able to figure it out."

"Marissa?" No.

"Oracle." Bingo! I was in! I should've known.

Chapter Sixteen

Nonny

Unfortunately, I had to use Mary's car to get to the airport after all. I had scribbled a quick note that I would be back soon and not worry. I would be smart about seeing my parents, and if anything were up, I would be on the first flight back to Peebles. Still having three hours before the plane would even leave, I thought about the earlier hours and the steps I'd taken to get to the chair where I now sat, waiting.

The ticket had been easy. One-way to Spokane. I would have to drive the short distance to Lewiston in a rental car. I packed a suitcase with my things and quietly left in Mary's car. The hard part was going by Mandy's house. I turned the headlights off and drove slowly, as far away from her house as I could. I didn't see any movement or lights, so I figured I was in the clear.

I had enough gas to make it here and had decided long-term parking would be a better option to leave Mary's car in. Mandy might have someone get it while I was gone, anyway. Who knew?

I was exhausted and cold. The office had been cold, and Mary's heater in the car had blasted hot air from the vents, but I hadn't felt it. I had dressed warmly, but I wondered maybe I was getting sick with the headache from earlier and the body chills. I couldn't wait for the airport to have a little life in it so I could check in and get some hot coffee. But, unfortunately, that wouldn't be for another hour, at least.

The anxiety I felt was shown in the bobbing of my knees up and down. A warm bed sounded terrific, even though I doubt I could've slept.

"Focus on the task, Nonny." Standing, I paced around a tiny area near the airline check-in counter.

"Are you okay, Miss?"

After jumping out of my skin and grabbing my throat, I calmed myself down enough to reply, "Y… yes."

"Sorry. I didn't mean to startle you." The voice belonged to an older lady who was dressed to the nines. What she would be doing here this time of night, herself I didn't know or care. She eyed me in not a pleasant way, being nosey.

"I'm fine. Just waiting for the check-in counter to open." I was still stammering my words.

The lady shook her head. "They don't let people on stuff fly. What are you on?"

"Excuse me? What? No! I'm not on anything! I'm eager to get back to the west and see my parents. It has been too long and…." I stopped. It was none of her business.

"Hmm. If you say so." She turned her nose up and didn't bother me with her unkind words anymore.

She left an icy chill in her wake. What was it with everything? Maybe I was going mad! She reminded me of someone, but I couldn't figure it out. Her demeanor and look weren't pretty but flawless; maybe if I spoke with her again.

I turned in the direction she had left and started walking. She couldn't be far.

Since the airport was still partially shut down because of the hours, I walked up and down the same hallways several times.

"Maybe she went to the bathroom or left." I tried the first bathroom. Nothing.

In the second one, I was surprised that she was now right in front of me after looking everywhere for her. She was staring at herself in the full-length mirror.

Raising her eyebrows at me, she leaned in toward the mirror and applied more lipstick.

"I… I…"

She stopped mid-motion and looked at me darkly as I stumbled once again with my words. "You? What?" she hissed crossly.

"Why did you approach me so unkindly?" I quizzed her.

"I had to see for myself. That's all." She had resumed putting on her lipstick.

"See what?" I shivered. The women's restroom felt like a meat-freezer.

"Do you know me?"

Did I know her? "No."

She laughed, throwing her head back. "Are you that dumb? Would you not remember meeting someone as," she paused, choosing her next word, "perfect as myself before?"

I shook my head, confused, very confused. "But, you asked me if I was okay, and then you assumed I was on something. Honestly, lady, I think you might be the one on something."

"You all are so stupid. So below the average… anything. I wanted to see for myself. And now, here you are, following me. So, what are you up to? Maybe you know more than you're saying?"

I didn't like the way she was looking at me.

"Did someone else get to you?" She moved toward me.

Instinctively, I moved a step back toward the exit.

"I just came to…." What? Talk?

"To what? Are the others here now?" She looked past me. I could see her face shift for a moment to fear, perhaps? It was quick, like a flash. Her eyes moved back to investigate mine.

"To talk. You seemed familiar. But after talking to you, I'm sure I don't feel that way anymore." I turned and ran out, looking to see if she would follow. She didn't, thank God!

People came to the airline check-in counters as well. All I wanted was to check in and get the hell out of this town. She certainly reminded me of a lot of dangerous vampires I previously met. Although I didn't see the general trademarks of the Drobny, I couldn't rule it out, either.

"Shit!" I hissed loudly under my breath.

"Excuse me?" The man ahead of me in line asked.

"Nothing. Sorry. I forgot to pack something." I stammered.

He nodded in commiseration. "I understand. It happens to me all the time." He turned back around as the attendant asked for the next person in line.

Surveying the area, I looked for the woman again, still nothing. My heart was racing.

* * *

The total trip took a little over twelve hours. With it being a last-minute booking, I had to stop in Dallas and Portland before reaching Spokane. West coast time was close to four. Once I got the rental car in Lewiston, I would have to decide what I would do tonight. My heart hadn't quit racing since the first lift-off out of Cincinnati.

In two hours, I would be home. "Home." My stomach fluttered. If only it were a pleasant routine visit with my husband and kids. "But you didn't choose that life, Nonny." Speaking to myself helped remind me that there was a lot more here at stake.

I had expected the actual meeting with my parents for twelve hours. The hugs and joys of being reunited, forgiving each other, and eventually forgetting the past. At least, that was the image I played over and over in my head. They were my parents, and I was their only daughter. Whatever the Drobny had done, I would make them realize. I would fix this and eventually make it all right. Finally, we would defeat Diamonté and his beasts and go back to Lewiston and live happily ever after.

"That will not happen." At least for the last part. Our children were a part of the Shadow Night. There was nothing I could do to change that.

"I want normal." You didn't choose normal, I reminded myself.

"I want my husband." Did he want me? Probably, whatever soulmate bond still existed in us. I missed him terribly.

"I want my children close." Well, you had Amethyst, but what about Jet?

"I want everyone home safe." And that was the problem.

* * *

The house was dark and unchanged. It seemed familiar and distant at the same time. I was across the street from it, and most of the block was still dark. It was daylight savings time and 6:30 p.m. The streetlights weren't on yet.

Should I go in and surprise them tonight? Of course! They were my parents and could be in the other room, watching a movie and eating dinner or something. It was a Saturday night, so it was possible.

I left the car and ran across the street. If I thought about it anymore and what would happen when the door opened, I might explode. Or get too nervous about doing just to it!

Ding-dong! The doorbell rang, and I waited like a schoolgirl, giddy with excitement. And then I waited some more, knocking loudly as well.

"Mom? Dad?" I put my mouth up to the crack of the door. Then, placing my ear against the wood, I listened. I heard nothing.

"Where on Earth could they be?" They were getting on in age, but they were not ancient by any means. Maybe they'd gone out to eat or something.

"I guess I could go check-in at a hotel and clean up a bit." It had been a long day, and I felt hungry and filthy. So turning, I headed back to the car and made a getaway to one of the nicer hotels in Lewiston.

Check-in was quick at the hotel, and after getting into a room, I made a beeline for the shower. My stomach rumbled. But a shower was needed. After that, I could order room service and then go back out and see if my parents were back home yet. They would probably want me to stay the night there after the hugging was all over. But the hotel room was handy for now.

I let the waterfall-like hot rain over me. The cold had consumed my body after leaving Ohio. The events of my day drifted through my mind, and I wondered how Mandy had taken the note. Probably not well. I thought of where Grant and the rest of the gang were. Certainly not as close as I was to the Sawtooth Mountains. They still had a few days of travel to face, I was sure. Jade would be a mess again. Funny how both her pregnancies had started in Ohio, and then she had a miserable trip on the road. It made me wonder if Grant and I could ever have more. I was nearing forty, but with kids like ours, I was confident that wouldn't matter.

Should I have tried the door or checked for the hide-a-key before leaving my parents' house? No. I'd made the right decision; at least that's how it felt. But, as much as I wanted everything to be okay between us, I had to face the fact that I might walk into a Drobny scenario.

My stomach rumbled again. The heat of the water had drained me. The adrenaline I had felt all day was drifting away. I yawned, wiping the steam from the mirror. I could throw my hair in a ponytail after eating. The room was a suite and was stocked with a soft white robe. I put it on after applying some coconut-scented lotion and brushing my hair out. I was feeling good. Hungry, but happy with where I was.

"I'm not a coward," I told the girl in the mirror and headed to the bed and nearby phone to place an order for food.

Shortly after that, with my stomach full of a cheeseburger, fries, and a chocolate milkshake, I let my eyes close for a second. I had to see my parents, but my eyes hurt so badly from staying open for so many hours. So, it would just be a second....

* * *

Waking up because of the light streaming through the windows, it took me a moment to organize my thoughts. "What?" I recognized the hotel room and remembered why I was there. "Damn it!"

"Damn it!" I said again. I had slept like a log all night long. Then, bolting up in bed, I threw the covers off.

"What time is it?" I looked at the clock. It was nine. "Nine?" I had slept for over twelve hours straight, and the room was as cold as an icicle. I threw myself back under the covers, not wanting to get out. Where was the damn thermostat in the room?

I made a run to it and read that it was only sixty degrees in the room. "Shit!" My teeth chattered. Sixty felt like twenty below! I ran back and threw the covers over my head. "Shit!"

I could get ready quickly. Shower and get the bathroom all warm and steamy, then get ready. Or I could wait about ten minutes for the room to heat. I settled on staying under the covers, allowing only my arm to reach out enough to get the remote control to turn on the TV. I hadn't watched the news here in ages. It might be good.

Eventually, the room warmed up, and I got ready. I wasn't hungry yet, but a hot cup of coffee from the downstairs barista sounded terrific. I also contemplated calling my parents on the phone. But I thought a surprise would be best. A face-to-face meeting would be best. I was feeling anxious again about the unknowns. What if…

"Damn, Drobny. Curse you all." For sure!

Thinking of my little family again, I said a brief prayer to keep them safe and that we would all be together soon.

The drive was quick, and once again, I sat outside my parents' house. I watched for a moment, hoping I would see them emerge from the house.

"I guess it's time." Swigging the last of my coffee down, I left the car behind.

Ding-dong! I rang the doorbell, just as I had the night before. However, this time I heard the shuffle of footsteps before the door opened to show a woman's face that wasn't my mother's.

"Yes?" She was probably around the same age as my mother, but was not my mother.

"I, uh, I'm looking for my parents. Jay and Beth Young? They live here. I used to live here?" So this was my old house, right? I stepped back a little and looked around. Yes, this was my old house.

The lady looked confused for a moment and then smiled faintly. "I remember the name as belonging to the people who owned the house before the people we recently bought the house from; it was just terrible…." She looked away awkwardly.

"What? What was terrible?" It felt like my heart was pumping in my throat and a knot was forming.

"Come in, child." The woman opened the door and took my hand, pulling me in.

"Come to the kitchen. I'll make tea. We can talk." Her voice was tender and sad. "You say you're the child of the original owners, and yet you do not know what happened to your parents?"

I followed. "I'm, it's complicated, but yes, I'm their daughter. I don't understand. Did something happen to them? Please!" I stopped her in the hall. She turned toward me. "Please, I've been away for so many years, unable to see or speak to them. It's complicated, as I told you." I could feel my eyes swelling with tears. "But we loved each other very much."

"Come, sit." She pulled me along. "I'll tell you what I heard."

Her kitchen table was our kitchen table. Looking around, I realized that a lot of the items were my parents'. I rubbed my hand over the table. Finally, the woman took a chair across from me.

"My name is Maxine, and I live here with my husband, Rex." We've been married for forty years and recently lost our home to a fire. The insurance money was enough to buy this place, fully furnished. Even the owners before us kept most of the furniture already here. We knew the history of this house, as we've been in the area for about ten years. But, well, the Drobny family had lived here for some time with their teenagers, so we thought it was all fine.

"Wait." My hand stopped her, and I looked up at her. "Drobny?"

"Yes. Did you know them?" Her eyes flashed around the room a bit like she didn't care to say the name either.

I nodded. "Unfortunately," I admitted. The tears didn't fall and the anger I felt heightened to an all-time high.

"My parents?" I needed to know.

"Well, this place sat vacant after the homicide, suicide." She spoke the words slowly, not wanting to upset me any more than I already was.

I forced myself to stay calm. There was no way that was what had happened here.

"Go on." I urged her.

"Well, they said the man, your father, I presume, went mad and shot his wife, and then, did himself in. I'm so sorry. What's your name?"

"Nonny."

"Yes, Nonny. I remember now. I'm sorry, Nonny., I know nothing else about your family. Just that, and well, the Drobny family purchased the house after everything got cleared up, lived here for a while, and then, well, they sold it to us." She paused, and I felt the tension in the room rise.

She whispered. "I think this house is haunted, Nonny. If we hadn't put all our savings into this place, we would get out of here."

I was sure it was haunted, but not by my parents. God rest their souls.

How could I tell her the truth? I couldn't.

"I'm sorry to have bothered you, Maxine. I don't… I can't…." Breaking down, I let the tears flow. Maxine came around and hugged me tightly.

"You aren't a bother, Nonny. God rest their spirits and bring you some peace. Can I get you anything? Do anything? Rex should be back soon." Maxine went and found tissues for me to use.

"Can I look around? My old room?" I whispered my request. I would understand if she didn't want me to, but I hoped she would.

"Of course. Stay as long as you like." Maxine patted my hand. "I'll be in here making some lunch.

Nodding, I got up on legs that felt like jello and headed for my old bedroom.

The window shades were still drawn, so the room was dim, but with plenty of sunlight still coming through the cracks. All the old furniture was still there, and it still looked very much like I remembered it. The room, though, felt empty, and it made me feel more so as well. The bedspread and pillows were different, and all signs of a teenager living and laughing in this room were gone.

I moved through the room, touching each piece of furniture, running my fingers over the tops, feeling the cold wood scales beneath, one by one. I moved to the bed and laid down, and stared at the ceiling, and I thought about what Maxine had told me. My parents were dead. Finally, the sobbing came now that the earlier shock had passed.

I cried for a long time, and when Maxine came in to check on me, I had curled into a ball and had found silence inside my aching heart. I was facing the realization that I had not only lost the only extended family I had, but could lose the rest I still had. My life felt dark and scary, and I didn't want to be left all alone in this world.

I felt the weight of Maxine's body sit down on the bed. Then, opening my eyes, I looked at her sad eyes.

"Where did it happen? Do you know?" I whispered my question to her. I wanted to know where my parents took their last breath.

"Their bedroom... my bedroom." Maxine corrected herself.

"May I?" Sitting up, I knew she would, but requesting permission seemed the right thing to do.

"Of course." Maxine got up and led the way.

My parents' room had not stayed the same. A complete remodel had taken place, and all the furniture was different.

"It has changed," I informed Maxine.

"Yes, after, well, there was a lot to fix." Maxine was hesitant to continue. Whether for my sake or her own, I wasn't sure.

"Why?" I watched the grimace on her face. She didn't want to talk about it.

"Things stir up when we talk of the past," Maxine said with much reluctance. "From what I was told, your dad destroyed this room, perhaps after he shot your mom and before he took his life. That's what the evidence said, at least that's what I was told." Maxine got ready to leave me to do what I wished in the room. "I have some lunch ready. Rex should be here any minute. I made a plate for you as well."

"Thank you. I'll be there in a minute." I hadn't entered the room, and I wasn't sure I would. There was nothing here that made me feel like my parents had been here. But there was a darkness in the air. It wasn't from my parents; I would bet my life on that.

The rest of the house seemed primarily unchanged. The furniture and incidentals were the same. These people had some of their items around, but not much. Maxine had stated everything had been lost in the fire. She had said that a box of pictures and a few miscellaneous items were all they could save.

Maxine and Rex were both quietly eating at the table. I hadn't heard him come in. He looked at me with wonder and pity, and I glanced at them both. They were probably older than my parents. Rex was bald with brown eyes, and Maxine had long white hair in a bun. Her eyes were also brown. They were a sweet couple who had lived a long life together, for sure.

"Nonny, this is my husband, Rex." He stood up and offered me a chair in front of the place where a plate sat holding a bountiful sandwich and a small bowl of soup.

"Thank you." I wanted to say it was nice to make his acquaintance, but it wasn't. Not on these terms anyway.

"I'm deeply sorry about your parents. It must have been quite a shock to knock at your own home and find out this way?" It came out as more of a question than a statement.

"Yes. I have been away much too long. Circumstances were unusual. But, as I told Maxine, we all loved each other very much. Despite what you might have heard." I wanted him to know my parents were not monsters, nor I.

"Do you have other family? To help you deal with this?" Rex wiped his mouth and waited for me to answer.

"Yes." I needed to finish chewing my mouthful of food. I wasn't the least bit hungry and the sandwhich was tasteless to me. I don't know how they thought I could eat or how I was going to choke down the entire sandwhich. "I have a husband and twin teenagers."

"Boys or girls?" Maxine asked.

"Both. A boy named Jet, and a girl named Amethyst." I sounded as proud as a mother should, no matter what the circumstances. They were my children, and where they were wasn't their fault.

"Oh, precious." Maxine smiled. "We have two older girls who have families and children and even a great-grandchild for us. But they don't come to visit nearly enough. Do they Rex?"

Rex didn't reply, just looked away.

"Are they far away?" I asked Maxine.

"One is in the Navy, and her husband is also in the Navy. Her name is Diane. And our older daughter, Carly, was here but moved to Spokane. Job promotion."

"Had we known she would get transferred, we would never have bought this house." Rex looked at Maxine. She agreed solemnly.

"Well, maybe you should sell the house, then?" I could certainly put the money up for it.

"We tried. No one wants it," Rex said.

"I'll buy it from you." Did I just throw that out there? Yes!

Surprised, they both looked at me. "This house is dark, Nonny. It would change you all. I can't do that. It was your house, but it's not what you remember." Rex wanted to sell it, but the good heart in him protected even me, a stranger, from whatever it was they were experiencing.

"Trust me. We could fix it." I placed my hand over his. Maxine looked at her husband with a plea in her eye.

"Listen. I have some things to do for my family. It won't be long. Find a place in Spokane, and let me take this place, my home, off your hands. Whatever you want for it, I'll pay."

"Rex?" Maxine wanted his attention.

"I… I don't know." Rex sat back, scratching his chin.

As far as I was concerned, I would start making everyone's lives right, starting here. Today!

Pushing my chair back, I felt bricks being lifted off my soul. "Get everything in order. Unless you want to stay?"

"No!" Maxine stood up.

"Maxine." Rex tried to calm her. "She doesn't know. She has a family."

"Exactly. This is my home. Please?" Rex and I stared each other down. I wanted him to see that it would be okay. This was my home, my battle.

"I don't know." He scratched his whiskered face.

"Say yes, Rex. Please?" Standing before him, I wanted this more than ever. I wanted to fix them and set this house at peace.

“You’re sure?” Rex asked.

“I won’t take no for an answer, Rex. For my family’s sake and yours.” I pushed my words at him.

He stood and nodded, stretching his hand out to mine. “If it means that much to you.”

Maxine was thrilled. “Praise God.” Now she was the one crying.

“It’s the right thing to do,” I told him, taking his hand.

“I won’t be gone too long. Get everything in order.” I walked to the front door, with both of them following behind me.

“You’re an angel, Nonny.” Maxine grabbed me in a hug, and her cheeks were wet with tears.

I smiled, but I wasn’t an angel. I was making things right. I had a morgue to visit now.

“I’ll be back soon. Make sure you cover your moving cost, furniture, whatever you need. Money will not be an issue.” I would have legalities to deal with from an heir’s standpoint, but that could wait.

“That won’t be necessary.” Rex took my hand and pulled me in for a hug. “Thank you.”

“It’s necessary. Figure it all out. I’ll be back in a few weeks at the most.” Then, pulling back, I needed to get going. My adrenaline had me on fire, and I had a lot to do.

With the last goodbye, for now, I was on my way to the morgue. I hoped that there had been a changing of the guard there. If not, I would attempt to find Grant’s old friends some other way.

* * *

The visit to the morgue was partially successful. I could locate two I sought among the many dangerous vampires there. I met with them that night at my hotel, finding out the Drobny part in my family’s death. Only they didn’t know the story as I knew it.

Talking with them in my hotel room made everything clear to them, and they swore on the Shadow Night that they would not return to the morgue but would seek out Hemi and the other soldiers. Life was on the line again. Only this time, no one had known.

How they would get through the blanket of the spell cast by Diamonté, I would probably never know. But they were determined and bid me farewell while they tried to bring order, hopefully for once and for all, back to the Shadow Night.

They also instructed me on how to get to the base of the Sawtooth Mountains to make it to the 'Drobny death palace,' as the three of us had named it. I would start in the morning and stand with my family for the fight of our lives.

That had been the plan; had the Drobny not followed Grant's friends and kidnapped me that same night. I couldn't tell you how sick of being kidnapped I was. Shit was about to get real.

Chapter Seventeen

Mary

The travel took its toll on Jade. Even Amethyst wasn't sure what to do anymore. She turned to the Higher Powers for help. But what could anyone do? Leave her with other people we couldn't trust at a time like this? Not an option.

We were close to the Sawtooth Mountains. I did not know exactly where we were going, but I stayed alert for the plan and Jade's needs. Amethyst kept quiet and to herself for the long journey across the U.S. When Tristan and Grant would go hunt, sometimes Jade accompanied them. She had a few good hours here and there. But, God bless a pregnant woman or vampire in this case. She didn't go out and run with them, but she dined with them. That was close enough for me. Amethyst, with her change of rank, became no more human or more vampire. She was spiritual and godly, and like everything I remembered when it had been me in that role. Dining on only products of the Earth, she was very much a vegetarian now.

Grant figured it out even before Tristan. The secret couldn't be kept, and Grant wasn't sure whether to be mad or happy. I told him to be happy. He worried about her having a life such as mine had been. But, no matter what he thought or felt, it was destiny and not his to dictate.

Amy and I sat at a small creek where the water ran hot and cold from the natural hot springs. We were near a small town named Atlanta, Idaho, where no gas station was to be found. The Sawtooth Mountains poked out of the side of the trees, away from us. By far, it was the most glorious vision I had ever seen. I'd always thought a mountain was a mountain, right? Wrong, I had been wrong.

The tall tops screamed danger with their angled peaks, and they mesmerized with nothing but beauty from a distance. But, to know what lived within them, somewhere, it was all wrong. The Drobny, Keegan, Diamonté, they didn't belong there or anywhere but in the bowels of Hell.

"Mary?" Amy chimed at me like a song. "Where are you?"

"I'm here. Just thinking." I nodded at the view. "Amazing, aren't they?"

"Yes. The negative energy that flows from it, though, makes it, I don't know. Haunting?" Amy wrapped her arms around herself. "I can feel Jet. It has been a long time since that happened." She whispered, so if anyone were near, hopefully, they would not hear her. "It's all different this time." Her hand moved up to the necklace around her neck and she caressed it softly.

I nodded, understanding her now more than ever before because of the Oracle Powers that flowed through her body. I wanted to be jealous of what she was feeling, but I couldn't be that way for her to succeed. She needed my knowledge and support.

"You have an amazing light inside of you now, Amy. I should know."

"I'm sorry for your loss, Grandmamma." Amy reached out to me, then pulled back, frowning.

"You need to take the red vial quickly, Grandmamma." In an instant, she pulled all her amethyst stones out and placed them in a small circle around me, each one touching the next.

"It's in the car. What's wrong?" The hairs on my neck rose on end.

"It's Jet. He is trying to do something. He knows something isn't right." She looked at the wooded area, evidently hoping the others would be there soon. "Where in the car?"

"In my purse. The pouch is in there. Just bring me all of it." Amy nodded and left me in my circle. I felt exposed, not safe. The wilderness could be unkind.

Amy returned shortly with my pouch. "Are we safe, Amy?" She handed me the bag, and I removed the vial. Should I take all of it? Some of it? I didn't know. I had been in an altered state before, and it didn't seem to have lasted all that long.

"I don't know. I can't be sure. I hear whispering, but I don't know if it's them or us." Good vs. evil. I was so done with the evil!

I drank it all and hoped for the best. Unfortunately, it didn't taste good. "How far?" I hoped it wasn't too far. Then what?

"There are secret passages all over the mountain. They don't like this area because of the hot springs here, but a passage is not too far away. You'll be okay." Amy reassured me.

"It didn't last all that long the first time." I shook my head, frightened of being so close to death in my altered state, with Keegan so nearby.

Amy placed her hand over my heart and closed her eyes. "Amazing." She felt the steady beat slow and finally stop. My breathing was no longer required, but I did it anyway. My body longed for the air to explode into my lungs.

"Does it hurt?" Her hand was still against my chest. "No," Amy answered herself.

It felt like she had touched my soul. I placed my hand over hers. "I'm so proud of you. No matter what happens, just know that." Amy smiled.

"You'll always be near me, Grandmamma," Amy said as she kneeled to collect her stones.

"Finally." Amy stood with her stones and motioned to the forest. "They're coming."

Soon, the three of them emerged from the woods. Jade looked like death as they carried her between them.

"Something's wrong," Tristan shouted to us.

"What do you mean?" Amy and I both ran to help them.

They placed Jade on a fallen log. “Jade, honey?” I touched her brow. “She’s warm. Why is she warm?”

“Mary,” Jade whispered. “Mary.”

“Jade, what happened?” I coaxed her to tell me, smoothing her hair down. Amethyst took her stones back out and placed them in a larger circle around us all. I felt a little tired but relaxed, as the others seemed to be as well. Amethyst stood outside of the ring. “Give her your energy, not all, but just enough.” She kneeled then and prayed.

“It was the blood of the beast.” Jade whimpered as she fed off the energy we extended to her.

“Jet… he knows or thinks he knows.” Amy stood and acknowledged me. “Jade was still feeding when he cursed these woods. We don’t have a lot of time to surprise them. I’ll do what I can, but we have to go if your plan is going to work.” Amy started gathering her stones so we could leave.

“What about Jade and my child?” Tristan asked Amy. He no longer saw her as some teenager. Instead, he knew she was to be listened to and honored.

“Safe and well as can be. We have little time. Please…” Amy looked at Grant, her father, but also her ally. “Now.”

He nodded and scooped Jade up by himself. “Tristan, get the car started, and let’s fly.” He set Jade in the back of the van. “Hang in there, Jade.” I heard him tell her.

Amy set her stones all over the inside of the van. “I want to shield us as much as possible,” she explained.

* * *

It was utterly silent in the van, right up to the secret passage. We didn’t hash out the plans again or try to predict what we might encounter. It was a done deal. We were knocking on the door.

“Mom?” Grant turned with an expression of wonder on his face.

“What?”

“How can you be sitting here alive but feel so dead?” He had figured out my heart wasn’t beating.

“The quest has many protocols.” I winked.

"What?" He questioned back.

"Good Lord, child." Feeling light at the moment, I reassured him. "The smoke people have a few things up their sleeve, still."

He thought about that, nodding. "What else?"

I shrugged. "I don't have the faintest. I just did as told on that one."

"Great." He turned around. The smoke people, he knew, were never good with answers.

Amy groaned. "He is so dark, but they control that." She was speaking, of course, of Jet. "I don't want to hurt him." She rubbed the necklace. "Please, nobody hurt him."

"What about Micah?" Tristan asked from the front of the van as he drove, diligently looking for anything out of the ordinary. Grant also scanned the mountainsides, looking for danger.

"Pullover, Tristan, quickly! There! Into the trees!" Tristan let questions slide and did as asked. Amy adjusted her stones and prayed. We all sat quietly, watching the road.

Three Drobny soldiers came around the bend on motorcycles. They didn't slow down, thankfully.

"How could we not hear them?" Grant questioned aloud.

"It doesn't matter. Go, Tristan, quickly. Jet and Micah are away from the main palace site, luckily. Don't ask me how I know this. But I've put us at risk. I had to know. I had to know." Amy said in a monotone.

"Where, Amy? How far?" Tristan was looking in the rear-view mirror at her as he tried to drive.

"I… I'm not sure… there're a couple of places. They stayed the night together." Amy said flatly.

Tristan and Grant looked at each other. Tristan looked like he was going to kill him. So much for the task at hand.

Tristan hit the steering wheel and jerked the van to a stop. Tristan glared at Grant. "That's my daughter!"

"Well, it's not like they're biologically related, right?" Grant said. "You can't help who you love."

"This shit isn't love! It's dark and wrong!" Tristan shouted. "She needs to find a true full-blooded soulmate!"

"Boys." I had heard enough.

"I'm going to kill him, and then you," Tristan shouted again.

"Boys! Tristan!" I shouted, hurting my voice.

While I had their attention for the moment, I reminded them, "We are in a life storm right now, and by God, so help me, Tristan, you'd best remember that. Amy didn't say that to hurt you, but to give you the facts we have. Now pull your head out of your ass so we can put life back in good order. You do not know what is real and what isn't at this point. I would advise you to remember, that man sitting right there next to you would give his life for you, and you would do the same for him, right?"

Both guys looked at each other. Tristan was looking hard at Grant. His posture finally relaxed. "Sorry, brother. This is all getting way out of hand and into my head."

Grant patted Tristan's shoulder. "We'll work this out later. Let's get our teenage rebels back under our roof and deal with all of that later."

"Agreed," Tristan said and drove on.

Relief settled within me, and we could get our minds back to the real danger at hand.

"Mary, that was well said," Amy whispered to me. I smiled and looked back to see how Jade had taken the news. She was lying on the seat curled into a ball, as much as her tummy would allow.

"Jade?" I asked as I stroked her shoulder. "You okay?"

She mumbled a small yes. That was good enough for me right now. She had worse things to deal with than a daughter who might be in love.

"I think we should split up," Grant said.

"I don't!" I answered for everyone in the van, I thought.

"No, listen. You all go on in here, and I'll try to head Jet and Micah off."

"I don't know. Amy's not sure where they are," Tristan said.

"I know the direction." She pointed. "Follow that trail, quickly. Jet won't know what to think. Do your best to throw him off."

Grant nodded and jumped out of the van before it even stopped. "See you all real soon." He shut the door and was gone in a flash.

"I hope it is real soon because I don't have a dagger this time to deal with the bullshit," Tristan growled.

"Mary, can you come to sit up here and keep an eye out?" Tristan looked back at me.

"Yes, of course." I moved carefully because of the sway of the van on the dirt roads.

"I don't know how much help I'll be, though." My eyesight wasn't all that keen either anymore.

"You'll be fine." Tristan touched my elbow. "I'm sorry for everything, Mary."

Well, that was candid.

"We all get a little testy from reality from time to time." Even me.

"There doesn't seem to be a lot of Drobny in the area. I wonder how we got so lucky." Tristan remarked.

"I think they are all at the Shadow Night," Amy said sadly. "This was only a temporary home, and even though they want us to think there are a lot of them, there aren't."

"Oh… hmm." Tristan thought about this latest information. "Stupid spell."

"Yes." Amy chipped in.

"They are not alone, Micah and Jet," Amy said after we went around a few more corners.

"Grant?" I asked.

"No. I'm not sure. It isn't my father, though, I would know. But, it doesn't feel hostile, and it doesn't feel right. So, I think there's something else going on here."

"Shit," Tristan said as he drove a little further.

"I'm going to put these amethyst stones with Jade. Our shield will be gone, but knowing that Jet is not at the palace yet, I think it's okay.

Jade sat up at hearing her name. "Thanks, Amy. I think they'll be what I need so I won't ruin everything." She sounded hopeful.

Tristan parked as we were near enough to walk the short distance to where all our fates waited.

Jade looked well, with the stones hidden in all her pockets and one in each hand.

"Ready?" Tristan asked us.

We all nodded as we walked through the forest, still trying to stay hidden.

Voices could be heard from our left, and we all stopped to listen.

"It's Grant and them…."

Several extra figures passed across the clearing ahead of us. If Grant was scared, he certainly didn't show it. Micah and Jet were hand-in-hand. Then the people Amy had mentioned but didn't know, we recognized.

"Hemi!" Tristan whispered louder than he'd planned. Hemi looked but didn't see us. Tristan turned around. "How did they know? What are they doing here?"

We shrugged, as we didn't even know whose side they were on. Hemi was there with several other Shadow Night soldiers.

"Maybe Keegan and Diamonté aren't even here. They would blast everyone by now for sure, to keep Jet." Tristan looked confused.

It was like Tristan saying his name touched my soul. "He's here," I whispered. "Trust me. They may count all the chickens they can get into the hens' nest before they…."

Tristan looked away. He didn't want me to finish. I couldn't blame him, and I felt the same.

"What do we do?" Amy asked.

"I was going to ask you that same thing," he answered.

“Smoke people?” Tristan looked back at me for help. I shook my head. However, again, I had the notion that I needed to remember what they’d said. Then, I would know when I needed to, at least I hoped so!

The palace wasn’t what I had imagined. In my head, I had envisioned one much like the Shadow Night’s because that was all I had ever known. However, this one was much different, and all that could be seen was an entrance into darkness. There was no beauty in it at all.

Grant stopped at the gates that circled the entrance. He spoke to Jet and Micah for a moment, then they nodded and entered without him. The simple fact that guards didn’t even line the entrance made me nervous.

Hemi stood outside with Grant while the others followed the rest. Then the two of them walked around, acting like they weren’t sure what direction to go. Tristan moved away from us without even saying a word. The rest of us just kneeled lower and waited. Tristan had something up his sleeve.

Amy stood up slightly and almost shrieked. Hemi grabbed her and covered her mouth just before she shouted out in surprise.

“I found Hemi and the guys before I found Jet and Micah. We have a plan in motion. They know… I don’t have the complete story, but Nonny is in Lewiston.” Grant supplied the information quickly as Hemi and Tristan looked on. And boy, did Grant look happy, knowing Nonny was nearby.

“She must have had a change of heart.” I patted him happily. Good for Nonny!

“Jet knows.” Amy insisted and changed the subject.

“I told Jet that you were behind me by another day. He seemed relieved, saying that the rest would all be back tomorrow.”

“How was Micah?” I asked for Tristan’s sake if he hadn’t asked already.

“Fine.” He didn’t want to say more. That was probably smart, and Tristan let it go at that, too.

“The guys are all setting up inside. Of course, there are a few of them. But, I think the masterminds are here,” Hemi stated.

“They are,” I assured him.

“There’s movement. We should probably go in.” Hemi looked at Grant.

"Tristan, stand by here. I'll somehow make it known when it's time for your safe entrance." Hemi looked at Jade as she stood up. The look of shock on his face was almost funny.

"Oh shit. Are you pregnant? Now?" He asked the dumb question.

Jade shrugged. "As if I planned it this way. I'm fine. I'm determined, and you need me."

"Okay." It was all Hemi said, and he turned with Grant to leave.

"Remember, wait for our signal," Grant whispered loudly.

After they left, Amy asked Tristan. "What if too much time goes by and it's because something has happened, and then we're doomed?"

"This is coming from an Oracle? Come on now, Amy. I can't have that from you." Tristan didn't like the negative.

"I'm just saying," Amy said. "Sure, it will be fine, but we never did the 'what if?'"

"There's no what if, that's why." Jade sounded better than she had the entire trip. Amy should've used the stones a long time ago.

The pouch was getting sweaty in my hands. I felt my heart lurch.

"Ugh!" I placed my hand on my chest.

"Time is not on our side today." but If I didn't have to see Diamonté, I would be all the happier that wasn't the case. The pain would start, and I would be discovered in no time.

Amy touched me. "They want me to tell you; you're stronger than you think." Amy closed her eyes and put her hands in the air. She opened her eyes after a moment and smiled at me as she brought her hands down.

Taking my hand, she turned my palm over and dropped my essence crystal into it. "Don't forget." I looked at her in bewilderment.

"How?" When had it been taken from me?

"I love you, Grandmamma." But there was sadness in her eyes that I didn't understand.

A loud disruption from the entrance of the palace disrupted our heart-to-heart talk.

A soldier from our team came running out, screaming, "Now! Now!" before dropping dead.

We didn't pause to react. Instead, we ran full speed to the entrance. Hemi appeared at the gate, thankfully with a Drobny now dead at his feet.

"It has begun. I hope you know what you're doing." Hemi looked like he had already been through hell and seen the other side.

We ran in to find ourselves in the heart of a massive foyer with a set of staircases on either side of us, rising to a balcony. Grant was staring up at Nonny, who was in Keegan's clutches. Micah and Jet stood between him and Diamonté.

"Well, if it isn't a family reunion, after all. And here I thought it was Jet telling a lie. I thought I was going to have to kill him rather than keep him.

"Micah!" Tristan hollered at her. She didn't even flinch at her name.

"She's not right, Tristan." Couldn't he see that?

Diamonté hadn't taken his gaze from me. "Hello, whore." he said, as nasty as ever. This time it was my turn not to flinch.

"And the one who got away." He took his stare off me just enough to look at his granddaughter, Amethyst. "I never thought I would have my whore, son, and two hell-beings all in the same room. All my mistakes."

"Can I kill this one yet?" Keegan asked Diamonté as he licked his snake-like tongue over Nonny's cheek. Nonny shrieked, and Grant lurched to get up the stairs, Hemi at his heels.

"I wouldn't if I were you," Diamonté warned him.

Keegan waved a dagger, much like the one we had used on him. "Remember this? Well, Rand doesn't have it anymore." Grant stepped back. "Where is Rand? Does anyone know?" Keegan's laugh turned into a hellfire screech.

"Enough!" Diamonté yelled at him.

Keegan looked pissed that he had hushed him.

Jet had remained quiet, but he didn't look as comfortable as he had when we'd first entered. I hoped he had heard and listened to what Diamonté was planning. If he thought he would live through this day, should Diamonté win, he'd better think again.

"Jet," Amy called out to him. Oracles, we think alike.

"Shut up!" he yelled back at her.

"Aw. Bring the sister up. Jet would like another crack at killing his sister since he didn't master it before he was born." Diamonté ordered Amy upstairs.

"Don't!" Grant told her. Nonny screamed in pain again.

"Kill her," he told Keegan.

"No, wait!" Amy shouted and pulled out of our reach. "I'm coming."

Amy climbed the stairs as quickly as she could. Keegan's knife now had a trickle of blood running down the blade.

Once Amy reached the top, she slowed her pace, unsure of what to do.

"Come here," Diamonté spoke to her. "I want to see you up close."

Amy stood before Diamonté. He sniffed her, looked at her, touched her, and then looked at me. "Well now, how does it feel to be dying?"

"Wonderful. I'll be rid of you, once and for all." I mocked him.

He growled, quite pissed off. "And now, the Shadow Night has no protection. So sad."

He hadn't picked up on Amethyst. I said a silent prayer of thanks. He put his arm around her, and Grant looked toward the stairs again.

"Ah-ah-ah." Diamonté shook his finger. "We still have a lot to talk about before you all die, well, most of you." He looked across from Jet at Micah.

"And Jade… How does your family fare now? Expanding, I see." He laughed at his joke.

"We are the same family, you idiot!" Jade yelled. "How could you do that to your brother? My mother and my brothers!"

"Touché… Jade… touché… I'm finishing what your father started." He stated the last part in anger. "I didn't start this!"

"But you did!" Jade retorted.

"Let me tell her." Keegan hissed excitedly.

"You want to discuss family affairs, Jade?" Diamonté looked at Keegan. "Go ahead."

Keegan wrapped his dagger-holding hand around Nonny and then pulled Micah to his side. Jet looked quite angry. Diamonté glared at Jet when he saw Jet move toward Micah.

"Stop and stand still," Diamonté warned him.

"She's mine," Jet demanded. Diamonté backhanded him.

"Shut up, I said." He demanded that Jet comply.

Jet glared at him but stood still.

"Jade, come on up here, and make this a real family reunion." Keegan ran his tongue over his lips. "You remember."

"No! No, I don't," Jade whispered back.

"What's he talking about, Jade?" Tristan held Jade's arm so she couldn't go anywhere.

Keegan caught Jade's eyes in his blank stare. "Come. Now."

And Jade tried. Her feet moved, but Tristan held tight. Nonny struggled with Keegan, probably thinking he would lessen his grip on her. Instead, he slashed her cheek and threw her to the side like trash.

"Come get your bitch!" he yelled at Grant. "You all won't be out of here anytime soon."

Grant wasted no time in running up the staircase and pulling Nonny into his arms to safety. But it wasn't time for joyous reunions.

"Quit, Keegan!" Tristan yelled.

"But, I don't want to, Tristan. She's mine as much as she is yours." Tristan faltered at the comment but held tight. Jade struggled with him in a dazed state.

"Micah. She's as much mine as she is yours. Isn't she Diamonté? Tell him." Keegan looked to Diamonté to support his revolting claim.

"No!" Tristan yelled. "Jade is my wife, and Micah is our daughter. She was blessed to us! Soulmates!"

"Soulmates… tell her, Diamonté."

"Micah's soul is cut in half. You and your idiot Elders; they know the rules, the law, and the way of being blessed in Royalty more than anyone. Jade is who she is, and cloaked or not for many years. It gave me opportunities to mess with inhuman nature, as I like to call it. So, you want to kill her now, Tristan? Micah is a part of you as much as she is a part of Keegan." Diamonté smirked.

"No! I can't believe it! I won't!" We all stood still, frozen in disbelief.

"Believe it or not. It doesn't matter to me. Keegan thinks it will help him get the girl, and maybe he's right, hmm? The wife, the daughter, and, oh, let's not forget about the son she carries. Keegan, you always said you wanted a son." Diamonté laughed at his remark.

"Not that one. I can take care of that one." He motioned a slit to his throat. "I don't take damaged goods. But, you can let go of my woman."

"No. Never!"

A barking came from outside and started getting louder and louder as he entered the gates.

"Well, who brought the dog?" Diamonté smiled. "I haven't had a real pet in well, never."

The dog, Kade, entered and ran up the stairs. It was like watching a movie in slow motion. Amy looked at me and looked up, reminding me it was time.

"Ciantaramo!" I yelled, and the feathers poured from the pouch, and I flew like a bird up to the upper level. In one grasp, I pulled the necklace from Amy and broke it into a thousand pieces. Then, I took hold of the vampire that had held me, hostage in so many lifetimes. He was frozen, his eyes bulging from their sockets. Keegan could only watch as Micah fell from his grasp, and Kade, in his dog-like state, sunk his teeth into Keegan's throat. He couldn't even scream. He toppled backward to the ground with Kade stuck fast to his throat.

I stood next to Diamonté and pulled the essence crystal from my pocket, as I had only one thing left to do.

"I love you all. Live in peace and know I'll always be with you." I threw the crystal high into the air, and prisms flew from it like a beautiful fireworks show.

Grabbing onto Diamonté, I looked at Kade, who still held Keegan by the neck but had turned to watch and wait for me.

"Jet, Micah, you're released. Drobny and their kind are gone forever." Micah snapped from her trance and clung to Jet in fear.

I blew a kiss to Amy, who smiled and gave a small wave. "Don't be far, Grandmamma."

"No, darling. Never." I told my beautiful granddaughter.

Kade and I were swept into the light of a thousand prisms, leaving only the light and love behind us.

Did darkness ever really have a chance?

I could see Grant look on in disbelief as he cradled his injured wife. The look in his eyes was a look that would comfort me forever. A glimpse of love and disarray, as he watched his parents disappear from his life forever.

Epilogue

Jade

It was the first time we had returned to Lewiston since Nonny and Grant had purchased her parents' home from Maxine and Rex. She wouldn't come until we could all travel, even our newest arrival.

Our son, Elijah, had been born hours after we arrived back at the palace. He was kicking and screaming and full of life, with striking features only comparable to his adoring father, Tristan.

Jet and Micah, well, it had been love. But it was more than just their hearts; it was spiritual. Micah wasn't anything but a miracle. We left what was said about her fathers-times-two in the past. She was the apple of her only acknowledged father's eye. Period.

And Amy was beautiful and studied hard, perfecting her role in helping protect the Shadow Night as the new Oracle. We would catch her talking aloud to the air when she thought no one was paying attention… Mary wasn't far, as promised.

Kiryana had never been seen or heard from again. Perhaps her soul had somehow crossed into the darkness by her choice. All we knew was she vanished with the rest. There were still many unanswered questions, and I wasn't sure if they would or could ever be explained. Sometimes it's better to leave stones unturned. Perhaps this was one of those times to let the Drobny and anything to do with them be forgotten.

The one question that would haunt us was why Nonny's parents were killed. What happened? Grant promised Nonny he would not rest until he had the answers for her.

We had first taken flowers to Nonny's parents' gravesite. Then we all had a few words and tears to give. The graves were now marked with the most beautiful headstones in the cemetery.

The sweltering summer day had turned the skies into a dark purple while we were at the cemetery. We were in for a treat but weren't sure what. I watched Nonny shiver as she felt the drop in temperature hit her so fast.

Tristan and I stood in Nonny and Grant's backyard as the shimmering snow fell. The moment became surreal. Smiling and hugging my husband and son close, it occurred to me; it was finally a new beginning for us and a peaceful goodbye to those we'd loved and lost as a blanket of summer snow softly fell upon us.

The End

About the Author

Molly Jauregui

Passion with the pencil in hand began at a young age for me. I wrote songs, played the guitar, and wrote poems to communicate my feelings. Children's books kept my inner child alive, and romances with a new twist for those with the bottomless need to read. Now a freelance writer living in Nevada with a couple of furry friends, Molly releases her final book *Unbroken* in the *Fated – A Vampire Trilogy.*

When I have a free moment I enjoy all things family. I have just started working with stained glass and love the artistic outlet I am learning. Of course books, books and more books!

Books by Molly Jauregui

Fated – A Vampire Trilogy

Awaken, Book I

Bound, Book II

Unbroken, Book III

Made in the USA
Middletown, DE
13 January 2022